Dear Reader,

Do you have a secret fantasy? Everybody does.
Maybe it's to be rich and famous and beautiful. Or to
start a no-strings affair with a sexy, mysterious stranger.
Or to have a sizzling second chance with a former
sweetheart.... You'll find these dreams—and much
more—in Temptation's exciting yearlong promotion,
Secret Fantasies.

Talented author Glenda Sanders brings this series to a
satisfying finale with her sexy, heartwarming story,
Look into My Eyes. Our heroine, Holly Bennett, faces a
terrifying dilemma. Her fantasy is to have a lifelong
commitment, a happily ever after. But she's fallen in
love with a man with no memory. Does she dare trust in
the power of their love—even though Craig's past
might put an end to their future?

Unfortunately, all good things must come to an end
and our Secret Fantasies promotion is now concluded.
We hope you enjoyed the "fantasy." Be sure to watch
for Temptation's exciting new promotions in 1996:
Rogues, The Wrong Bed and Mail Order Men.

Happy Reading!

The Editors
c/o Harlequin Temptation
225 Duncan Mill Road
Don Mills, Ontario, M3B 3K9
Canada

Dear Reader,

Books often begin when a writer asks herself the question, "What if?" But while working on *Look into My Eyes*, the question in my mind was a little different. For me, the catchphrase from the movie *Speed* fits this story better. Not *"What if?"* but *"What would you do?"*

As I wrote *Look into My Eyes*, I frequently asked myself that question: What would you do? What would you do if you were attracted to a man with no name, no past, no future—a man who was drawn to you as strongly as you were drawn to him, but who could make you no promises?

For me, the fantasy was believing that a woman could love strongly enough, that she could take her lover's essential goodness on faith. Face it, wouldn't we all like to believe that we could find that level of strength and nobility within ourselves?

The heroine of this book, Holly Bennett, finds that strength.

I enjoyed living this fantasy through Holly. I hope you do, too.

Happy fantasizing!

Glenda Sanders

It was the Big Bad Wolf

At least, Holly's visitor had ears like the
Big Bad Wolf. And she suspected that if she
looked, he'd have a bushy tail, as well.

Playing games, was he? She opened the door
as far as the chain latch permitted and said,
"My mother told me never to open my door
to wolves."

"Open the door and let me in, or I swear that I'll
huff, and I'll puff, and I'll blow the house in!"

"Or wake up all my neighbors," Holly said,
relenting. She'd been right about the tail. It
swished proudly behind him.

"I can't believe you—*Craig?*"

He grinned at her. "The name is Wolf," he said,
pulling her roughly into his arms. *"Big—"* He
nibbled on her neck above her pajama top.
"Bad—" His hands slid under her top to knead
her bare back. *"Wolf."*

He pressed her against the door and kissed her
as if he'd been waiting a century for the taste of
her. His mouth and hands were greedy and
restless, persistent and relentless. "Sweet little
girls like you shouldn't let wolves in," he
whispered as he kissed his way to the place
where her pajama top buttoned. "You could get
eaten up!"

While working on this book, **Glenda Sanders** says she was reminded that fantasies are merely dreams, and that dreams can come true. In fact, she was suddenly surrounded by proof. Her daughter's dream of opening a pet grooming salon recently became true, as did her son's hope of seeing his favorite basketball team make it to the NBA finals. Glenda's personal dream has always been to write books that readers love to read. Obviously, dreams can come true!

Books by Glenda Sanders

HARLEQUIN TEMPTATION

Don't miss any of our special offers. Write to us at the following address for information on our newest releases.

Harlequin Reader Service
U.S.: 3010 Walden Ave., P.O. Box 1325, Buffalo, NY 14269
Canadian: P.O. Box 609, Fort Erie, Ont. L2A 5X3

Glenda Sanders
LOOK INTO MY EYES

Harlequin Books

TORONTO • NEW YORK • LONDON
AMSTERDAM • PARIS • SYDNEY • HAMBURG
STOCKHOLM • ATHENS • TOKYO • MILAN
MADRID • WARSAW • BUDAPEST • AUCKLAND

ISBN 0-373-25666-3

LOOK INTO MY EYES

1

HE WAS STARING at her again.

Holly swallowed the lump of disquiet that had formed in her throat and forced her attention back to the picture book she was holding up. She read aloud: "'Who will help me grind my wheat?' asked the Little Red Hen."

She panned the sea of four-year-old faces gathered round her. "And what do you think the dog said?"

"Not I!" responded a chorus of young voices.

"And what do you think the cat said?" Holly asked.

She glanced down the aisle between collected short stories and single-title general fiction, where the new shelving assistant was putting books away. As though he'd sensed her eyes on him, he looked up and met her gaze with a bold intensity that made her feel, somehow, exposed. But as the children cried out rowdily, his gaze widened to include them, and he smiled in amusement at their antics.

The smile softened his features, making him seem less brooding . . . and more charming. Involuntarily, Holly's mouth twitched into an answering smile. Realizing it, she deliberately took her eyes from his face. She wasn't about to encourage him. Being handsome as the devil did not excuse bad manners. His stares were unsettling, and he was too . . . virile.

Glancing at the book to compose herself, she asked the children, "And what do you think the rat said?"

"Not I!" they shouted.

"You guys have heard this story before," she teased, turning the page and hoping they wouldn't notice how distracted she was by the man watching her from the stacks.

His name was Craig.

"'And who will help me make a dough?' said the Little Red Hen," she read.

It was only a name. Only a combination of letters. Only a coincidence that his name was the same as—

"'Not I,' said the dog."

She couldn't go through life avoiding men named Craig. Avoiding men who weren't named Craig. Avoiding men who weren't Craig.

"'Not I,' said the cat."

He looked nothing like the other Craig. *Her Craig.* This Craig was taller. Leaner. Less rugged. More handsome.

He was still staring. Holly took a deep breath as she turned the page. "'I'd be delighted to help,' said the rat," she improvised.

"No!" First one child, then others, protested.

Holly feigned confusion. "What's the matter?"

"That's not what the rat's supposed to say," answered a precocious little girl in denim coveralls. A dozen heads nodded in agreement.

"Then what does the rat say?"

"Not I!" the children shouted.

Holly glanced apprehensively at the stacks, but the shelving assistant was gone.

She'd overreacted, she decided. He probably hadn't been staring at *her*, at least not in the way her vivid imagination had interpreted his attention. He'd probably just noticed the commotion and been curious about what was going on. She suspected that he'd never worked in a library before and, like many people, had expected a library to be quiet and tomblike.

Story Hour with a dozen four-year-olds was seldom quiet, as the youngsters assembled around her, waiting with squirmy impatience for her to turn the page and continue reading, demonstrated.

She did not give the shelving assistant another thought as she finished the story, but as she told the children goodbye and collected hugs from the ones who attended Story Hour regularly, she happened to glance in the direction of the stacks and discovered him one aisle over from the one he'd been working earlier.

He was staring again.

She snubbed him, pointedly turning her back to field a question from a mother who'd come to collect one of the toddlers.

"WE SHOULD HAVE INVITED the Mystery Man to lunch," Sarah said.

Holly paused with her fork midway between her plate and her mouth. "The new shelving assistant? Why?"

"Why?" Meryl said, with a hoot of laughter. "Do you mean aside from the fact that he's male and gorgeous?" A divorcée in her mid-forties, Meryl was not shy about her appreciation of the opposite sex.

"It's been so long since Holly went out with a man, she's forgotten what it's all about," Sarah said.

The teasing barb cut deeply. "That's unfair," Holly said. "You know why—"

Holly observed the concerned looks that passed between her two closest friends and fellow librarians. God, but she was sick of those looks, of the admonitions to put the past behind her, of the sympathetic clucks and pep talks.

After a strained silence, Sarah spoke. "Enough is enough, Holly. It's time—"

"To let go? To get on with my life?" Holly finished for her.

"You can't go on—"

Holly sighed like a balloon deflating. "Sunday would have been my first anniversary."

"Oh, God!" Sarah said, tossing a desperate look at Meryl. "We didn't realize—"

"It's all right," Holly said, but the expressions on her friends' faces told her they were unconvinced. She drew in a fortifying breath. "In fact, I have an announcement to make."

She sensed her friends' curiousity as she paused for dramatic effect. Finally, she said, "I donated my wedding dress to a charity auction."

"It's about time," Meryl said. "You didn't need to see that dress every time you opened the closet. It wasn't healthy."

"It's a relief to have it out of the house," Holly admitted. "Besides, it was a beautiful dress. Someone should get some good out of it." *Wedding dress. Size eight. Custom ordered. Ivory satin and lace with seed pearl accent. Never worn.*

Meryl lifted her soft-drink glass. "To your first step!"

"Hear, hear!" Sarah agreed, raising her glass, as well. "It's about time!"

Holly acknowledged the toast with a nod. It was comforting to have the support and approval of her friends; what she'd done had not been easy.

She'd known, when Craig was killed in the line of duty, that she'd never wear the dress. She'd bought it to wear at Craig's side, and wearing it for any other man was unthinkable. But there had been a brutal finality in watching the volunteer carry the garment bag from her apartment. She'd been forced to accept, in her heart as well as in her head, that she would never see it again. That she would never stand next to Craig wearing it. That she would never become Craig's wife. That the future they'd planned together had died along with the groom.

"I packed up Craig's clothes, too."

She said it casually, as though folding his garments had not shredded her heart into little pieces, and seeing his shirts and jeans had not awakened memories so sweet and intense that she'd cried herself to sleep for two nights in a row. As though touching the fabrics that had clothed his flesh had not made her recall and yearn for the tender caresses and heated embraces they'd shared.

"You still had Craig's clothes?" Sarah asked, appalled.

"Not hanging in the front of the closet or anything. In drawers."

"I hope you got them out of your apartment," Meryl said.

"Close," Holly said. "They're in two plastic bags in the storage room."

Except for his shoes—the tattered joggers he'd worn for his daily run along the beach. Those, she'd packed, then plucked from the top of the bag at the last minute, unable to seal them away. They were in her closet now, far enough back on the shelf that she couldn't see them readily, yet close enough that she could be comforted by the knowledge that they were there.

"You should take them somewhere," Meryl said.

"I'm planning to take them to a homeless shelter," Holly said. "I just ran out of time this weekend." She took a sip of cola. "Can we talk about something else?"

"We could talk about the Mystery Man," Sarah suggested hopefully.

"Works for me!" Meryl said.

"I don't see what's so mysterious about a shelving assistant," Holly said.

Meryl scowled in exasperation. "When was the last time you saw a shelving assistant who looked like he walked straight off the cover of *GQ*?"

Holly shrugged. "There's no rule that shelving assistants have to be nerds. He's probably a student."

"He's too old to be a student," Sarah said. "Unless he's working on a Ph.D."

"Possible," Meryl said thoughtfully. "He's quiet, but when he says something, it's not 'Duh.'"

"I don't think he's a student," Sarah said. "He told Maggie he'd work as many hours as she needed him. With no schedule restrictions. If he were a student, he'd have to mold his hours around classes."

"Maybe he's writing a thesis," Meryl said.

"Maybe he saw a crime and now he's in the witness protection program," Sarah said.

"Maybe he *committed* a crime and he's in hiding," Holly suggested mockingly. "The witness protection program! You two have spent too much time in the mystery section. They list county jobs at the unemployment office, you know. He probably just needed a job and took the first thing that came up. And who wouldn't need extra hours with what they pay shelving assistants? He may have a mortgage hanging over his head."

"Not unless he *owns* that old Victorian house on the corner of Third and Maple," Sarah said.

"Third and Maple?"

"The one that's divided into five little apartments," Meryl said. "That's where he lives. He walks to work."

"He doesn't have a car," Sarah said.

"See why we call him the Mystery Man?" Meryl asked.

"Because he doesn't have a car?" Holly countered.

"Guys like him usually drive vintage sports cars or BMWs," Sarah said.

"Especially the ones who live on a shelving assistant's pay," Holly replied ironically.

"I can't believe you're not curious about him," Meryl said. "He's only the sexiest man to ever work for the library system."

"He's curious about her," Sarah said smugly.

"What do you mean?" Holly asked with an edge of alarm.

Sarah looked at Meryl and lifted her eyebrows. "The woman's totally oblivious." She turned to Holly. "He looks at you like you're the main course at Thanksgiving dinner."

"It's that obvious?" Holly asked.

"You *have* noticed," Sarah said. "Yes, it's *that* obvious!"

"He has the hots for you, toots!" Meryl said.

"I was hoping maybe he looked at everyone that way."

"Don't we *wish!*" Sarah said.

"Oh, we do. We surely do," Meryl agreed.

"So?" Sarah asked, addressing Holly after a brief silence.

"So what?" Holly asked.

"What are you going to do about him?"

Holly shrugged. "If he keeps staring at me, I'll have to talk to him."

"Talk to him?" Sarah's disappointment was evident.

"It's inappropriate," Holly said. "There's no reason I should be uncomfortable at work."

"Uncomfortable?"

"That's the way I feel when he stares at me."

"It's time a guy made you squirm a little," Meryl said.

"Not at work."

"There's no rule about library employees...*you know*," Sarah said.

"I have no intention of *you knowing* with someone I have to work with. Especially—"

"I think the lady doth protest too much," Meryl told Sarah.

Grinning, Sarah nodded. "You're right. He's getting to her."

"Why don't you give the guy a break and smile at him?" Meryl said.

After a pause, Holly snapped, "I couldn't go out with a man named Craig, all right?"

Sarah and Meryl exchanged horrified looks. For several seconds, no one spoke, but, finally, Sarah broke through the awkward silence by asking, "In that case, can we have him after you break his heart?"

Holly welcomed Sarah's infusion of humor into the tense discussion. Much to her relief, the topic of the new shelving assistant became lost in the confusion of dividing the luncheon tab and computing tips.

HOLLY'S PROBLEM with the shelving assistant was not so easily dispatched at work that day, when she discovered him staring at her again, this time from the biography stacks. He smiled sheepishly when she looked up from the paperwork she was doing at her desk, but he didn't try to pretend he hadn't been watching her. Holly decided to stare him down. Perhaps if she embarrassed him, he'd realize that she didn't appreciate his attention and become discouraged.

But he was not as easily discouraged as she'd hoped. Throughout the afternoon and evening, they replayed the same scenario, he staring, she staring back defiantly until he returned to his work. Then, an hour before closing, he entered the U-shaped preschool reading area where Holly was working.

"You look like you could use some help," he said.

Seated on the floor with picture books scattered all around her, Holly could hardly deny that she did. It was the first chance in several days she'd had to devote close attention to the section, and the shelves were in total disarray. "Yes," she said reluctantly. "I guess I could."

He shook his head as he surveyed the chaos. "I'm not sure I know where to begin."

Oddly, at close range, he appeared younger than from a distance. His hair curled haphazardly over his forehead with just a suggestion of rebellion. And though he was well over six feet tall and looked twelve feet high from Holly's vantage point on the floor, he didn't seem menacing in the least. He seemed...almost boyish, and genuinely perplexed by the mess left behind by the preschoolers.

His earnestness was endearing. Holly found it difficult to associate this man with the one who'd been gawking at her from the stacks. "It does look as though a tornado's gone through here sometimes," Holly said. "But if we can get kids to love books at an early age—"

"You'll have them Booked for Life," he said, quoting the slogan posted throughout the children's library area.

"That's the theory," she said.

A brief silence followed. Holly became aware of his gaze, not lewd by any standard, but inarguably male. Stiffening, she said authoritatively, "Each section of shelving is marked with a letter or letters. The books are arranged alphabetically by title."

"Disregarding the articles 'a,' 'an' and 'the,'" he said drolly.

Holly's eyes narrowed as she looked at his face. She had a niggling suspicion that he was mocking her. "Yes," she said firmly. "*Disregarding* the articles."

Picking up an armload of books, she instructed, over her shoulder, "I started with the A's. You can start with X-Y-Z and work backward. Pull any books that don't belong in the section you're working in and put them in the right section when you get to it."

"X-Y-Z it is," he said, with the same droll tone he'd used earlier.

The shuffle of footsteps, followed by the methodical clapping of book against book, told Holly that he'd found the shelf and begun sorting. She resumed her own work with renewed vigor.

Eventually, working from opposite ends, they both reached the shelves that formed the bottom of the U. He nodded amiably as he turned the corner, walking on his knees and pushing ahead of him the stack of misplaced books he'd culled from the sections he'd gone through. Holly returned the nod and went back to sorting, wondering why she hadn't told him to start with the M's and work to X-Y-Z so that they would not be moving inexorably closer together.

Pausing between sections to rub a kink out of her shoulder, she inadvertently looked in the direction of the shelving assistant and discovered him staring at her yet again. As disconcerting as his scrutiny had been from across the room, it was even more so at close range. From across the room, she had not been able to discern that his eyes were a deep, midnight blue.

Flustered, she snapped, "Is there a problem?"

He did not answer her immediately. Instead, he regarded her thoughtfully, as though he might find a suitable answer to her question on her face. Like Holly, he was sitting on the floor, and he draped his arm across his knee, letting his hand dangle. His fingers were long and slim.

Like his body, Holly thought. Long and slim and elegant. Give him a taut English accent and a black tuxedo and he could play James Bond.

"You've probably noticed me looking at you," he said at last.

She answered with a tight nod and lowered her gaze to the spines of the books she'd just straightened.

"I'm sorry if I made you uncomfortable. It's just—" The thought faded into a sigh. After a beat of silence, he said, "You look so familiar. Have we met before?"

"No," she said, risking a glance at him.

"Are you sure?"

The intensity of the question was more troubling than her annoyance at his doubting her certainty. "Yes, I'm sure," she told him.

"The feeling that I know you is so strong—maybe we knew each other—" he shook his head as he searched for a way to express himself "—a long time ago."

"I don't think so," she said. "I'm good with faces. I would remember if we'd met."

He nodded, and the gesture seemed so laden with desolation that Holly found herself adding, "It's an awful feeling, isn't it, thinking that you know someone, yet not being able to place them?"

"Yes," he agreed. "Awful."

Again, the intensity with which he spoke made Holly ill at ease. His gaze held hers captive, and as she looked into his eyes, watching with rapt fascination as midnight blue deepened to indigo, she sensed in him the same quiet desperation she'd harbored deep within herself since Craig's death. She felt a peculiar kinship with him, irrational but no less real simply because it made no sense. Was it truly loneliness she saw in his eyes, that desperate, hopeless loneliness that comes from losing someone you loved?

He probably cheated on his wife and she kicked him out of the house, she thought, feeling foolish for letting her imagination run amok. She deliberately shifted her attention to the books in front of her. Frowning, she plucked a book with a badly torn spine from the shelf and examined the damage, stroking the torn cloth with her fingertips.

"Looks like someone got a little rough," the shelving assistant commented.

Holly nodded. "I'll have to patch it up until I can get a replacement copy."

"Do you always replace the books that get torn up?"

"We try, especially when it's a popular title. Those are the ones that get all the wear." She put the book on the top of the stack she was accumulating for repair.

The shelving assistant picked it up and examined it curiously. "This one's popular, huh?"

"*Make Way for Ducklings?*" Holly replied. "It has been for over thirty years. It's a Caldecott winner."

He gave a short, self-deprecating laugh. "I'm afraid I don't know what that is."

"You should . . . if you're going to work in a library," Holly said. "It's an annual award for the best picture book. *Make Way for Ducklings* won it back in the forties or fifties. Didn't you read it as a child?"

For an instant, she saw sadness in the depths of his eyes, too profound to hide. Then he shrugged, feigning a nonchalance that belied what she'd seen. "It's been a long time since I was young enough for picture books."

Holly grinned. "I forget that not everyone feels the same way about books that I do. I can't imagine anyone forgetting *Make Way for Ducklings.*"

Abruptly, he slid the book back on the stack he'd taken it from and turned to the shelf he was working on. "If it's that popular, I must have read it, right?"

"Probably," she agreed, culling a misplaced book from the shelf.

"Maybe I'll read it again once you get it repaired."

She stopped her work to look at him. "Why?"

"To recapture my misspent youth, of course." He grinned, but the bitter irony of his words defeated the mischievous tone he was attempting.

A few minutes later, he'd progressed to the section of shelving adjacent to the one she was sorting through. Holly's senses prickled. She had not been this aware of a man since Craig's death. His knee was scarcely an inch away from her thigh, threatening to nudge it at the slightest slip. Holly wasn't sure whether she actually felt heat from his body, or was merely aware that he would be warm if he touched her, warm in the way men were warmer than women.

His elbow brushed her arm. For an instant, Holly froze. Then he spoke, and politeness dictated that she look at him.

"I, uh, guess we've met in the middle," he said. His smile, genuine this time, did wondrous things to his handsome face. Things that could do wondrous things to a woman's insides.

Reflexively, Holly smiled back at him. They had, indeed, met in the middle. Then, realizing how effortlessly he'd charmed her, she pushed the stack of books she'd pulled from the shelves in his direction. "Trade you my O to Z's for your A to M's."

The sooner they were moving in different directions, the better.

2

OLD SAYINGS, Holly thought, were not always accurate. Out of sight, for example, was not necessarily out of mind—at least, not in the case of a certain shelving assistant. The library was closed on Sunday, and Monday was her day off, so she hadn't actually seen him in two days, but he'd been very much on her mind the entire time. She had only to close her own eyes to see the midnight blue of his.

But what lingered hauntingly in her mind was neither the charming mischief that lit his eyes when he smiled, nor their frankly sensual gleam when he stared at her. It was the loneliness she'd glimpsed there. The confusion. The profound sadness.

She wished the opposite were true. Being attracted to a man was less complicated than being concerned about him. She was not ready for the emotional investment required in caring about someone. A little consensual, recreational sex—responsibly handled, of course—would be preferable.

Sighing, she sank into the plump cushions of her couch, where she'd been trying, unsuccessfully, to concentrate on a novel predicted to become the literary sensation of the year. *Since when do you indulge in recreational sex, responsibly handled or otherwise?* she chided herself.

The answer to that one was easy enough: Never. She'd never slept with a man she didn't care about deeply. She hadn't lost her virginity until her second year of college, and that relationship had lasted almost two years. Then there'd been only one other before she met Craig. Sex, for her, had always been an extension of deep affection; physical desire, a by-product of caring about someone.

Perhaps that's why the yearning had caught her so by surprise. At first, she'd just missed Craig, and all the things about him that made him who he was. His voice. The sound of his laughter. The texture of his skin. His expressions. The way he touched her.

Eventually, she'd begun to miss their lovemaking in a totally different way. Emotional pain and loneliness had gradually given way to a physical need that had her aching. For tenderness. For appeasement. For fulfillment.

She wasn't ready yet to care about someone or to make love. But the yearning was relentless. Perhaps it was time she tried recreational sex. With a suitable partner. Someone to whom she was attracted. Someone—

Someone whose name wasn't Craig.

Someone whose eyes weren't filled with a sadness that nagged at her like an unsolved riddle.

Holly shifted restlessly and reopened the book in her lap, determined to drive the image of the new shelving assistant from her mind, but the story, a dark tale revolving around family secrets and revenge, held no appeal for her. After a few minutes, she gave up on reading and, inevitably, her thoughts drifted to the one subject she was trying not to think about: the shelving assistant. Also known as the Mystery Man. It was an apt name for him, although not for the reasons the other librarians had assigned it to him. They were intrigued by the fact that he didn't drive and that he lived in a subdivided Victorian rooming house. Holly was haunted by the shadows of pain in his eyes.

Suave and handsome, he seemed the last person in the world who would be nurturing a deep, silent pain, yet with a single, lingering glance into his eyes, Holly had recognized the loneliness. The sadness. The sense of disorientation and alienation from everything that had once been familiar and comforting. What had put that sadness in those midnight blue depths? What demons taunted him?

Mentally, she squared her shoulders in resolve. Whatever demons he was wrestling were none of her business—and she wasn't about to let them become her business. She was too busy fighting her own nightmares—she couldn't take on anyone else's.

THOUGH IT WAS impossible to avoid the shelving assistant in the small library, Holly tried to establish an emotional aloofness that discouraged anything beyond a superficial, co-worker to co-worker relationship.

Midway through the week, she decided that her plan would have been easier to execute if the shelving assistant shared her agenda. He unfailingly followed up hello with an affable comment about the weather, or how crowded the library was, or how busy she looked. She responded with nods or one-word replies, determined not to let casual greetings grow into a lengthy conversation.

His watching her posed a greater challenge. She would be in the middle of something—filling out a book requisition form, or explaining to a child how to locate a particular book on the shelves—and look up to discover him staring at her from the stacks. The situation was disconcerting at best. Had he been a stranger, instead of an otherwise affable fellow employee, she would have been uncomfortable to the point of fear. But this was no stranger lurking in dark alleyways—it was Craig Ford watching her from the stacks.

It was probably his way of flirting, she told herself. When caught, he would lift his shoulders in a gentle shrug and smile sheepishly or, even more devastating to her resolve, make a silly face. Holly would shake her head and grin, only to realize afterward that she'd allowed his self-deprecating charm to niggle its way past her defenses when, by all rights, she should feel violated by his constant scrutiny.

During Thursday afternoon Story Hour, he was back in the fiction section, grinning as guilelessly as the youngsters gathered around her as she read about Peter Rabbit's close call in Mr. McGregor's garden. Holly pointedly ignored him. Knowing he was there, however, made her self-conscious as she read, and by the time Peter was back safe with his mother and siblings, she had made up her mind to put a stop to his skulking and staring, once and for all. The next time he tried to strike up a conversation, he was going to get one.

She didn't have to stew over her decision long. Half an hour before closing, he strolled into the reading corral and shook his head at the chaos. "Weren't these books in perfect order this morning?"

"There's been a lot of reading going on in here the last few hours," Holly said.

"A or X-Y-Z?"

Holly deliberated over the question before replying, "Go ahead and start at the beginning and work straight through. I want to check out some shelf-top display materials that came in today's mail."

Acknowledging the directive with a nod, he walked to the end shelf. Within seconds, he was straightening and sorting, his shoulder muscles straining against his shirt as he moved his arms. He appeared larger than life, out of proportion, as he sat on the floor next to the low shelf and shuffled through the slender picture books.

Holly sucked in a deep breath. "Craig—"

Why was it still so difficult for her to say the name?

He stopped his work to regard her with an expectant lift of eyebrow.

"There's something—" Holly suddenly reconsidered bringing up the subject of his staring at her. Although it was reasonably quiet and their conversation would be private, there was something ludicrous about the idea of confronting him in this lilliputian atmosphere of waist-high shelves and kid-size beanbag chairs. "Just pull the misplaced books and leave them on the floor. I'll come along behind you and shelve them when I finish with the displays."

She didn't wait for a reply before turning abruptly and leaving the reading corral to go to her desk. The display she'd received in the mail, a freestanding cardboard space station, was clever and appealing, but complicated to assemble. Holly became so involved with inserting tab A in slot A and tab B in slot B that she lost track of time. Before she knew it, the lights blinked and Meryl's voice came over the speaker system announcing that the library would be closing in five minutes.

Holly leaned back in her chair, rotated her head a couple of times to ease the tension in her neck muscles, then resumed work on the display. She was over halfway through with the model, so she might as well finish it before leaving for the day. She was still engrossed in the assembly, when Meryl approached her desk. "Are you going to stay much longer?"

"Ten minutes," Holly replied. "I've just got a few more of these tabs, then I'm going to dot the joints with glue so it'll be dry in the morning."

"Heather has a math test tomorrow," Meryl said hesitantly, referring to her daughter, who was a sophomore in high school. "She may need some help."

"You go on. I can close up."

"If you're sure—" Meryl's relief was evident.

"I'm sure," Holly said. Craig had never liked her to be the last one out of the library at night. He'd always insisted that he meet her there when she had to close, even if he was on duty. Ironically, his death had given her a fatalistic philosophy: if something awful was destined to happen, it would, regardless of anyone's actions. Instead of making her cautious, his death had made her reckless.

"Then I'm out of here!" Meryl said.

"See you tomorrow," Holly said distractedly as she began to work on the display once more.

Closer to twenty than ten minutes ticked by before the spaceship was fully assembled. Pleased, Holly leaned back in her chair to admire her handiwork.

"Need some help with that?"

Shrieking in surprise, she bolted straight up in the chair. "What are you doing here?" she asked, her heart in her throat.

"I work here," the shelving assistant said with an undertone of amusement.

"Until nine o'clock!" Holly snapped.

He shrugged indignantly. "I decided to finish the picture-book section before I left."

"Oh." Holly's heart was slowly sinking back into place.

"I'm sorry if I frightened you."

"I didn't realize you were still here."

"You were pretty involved in that spaceship."

"Umph!" Holly said, rolling her shoulder stiffly. "And I have the cricks to prove it."

"I could try to work them out for you," he offered.

Holly's scalp prickled with the realization that they were the only two people in the building. She gave him a quelling look. "I don't think that would be such a good idea."

"Just trying to help," he said, with a poignant sincerity that made her wonder, briefly, if she'd overreacted. He was so nice. Likable.

Serial killers seem likable, she thought. *Sociopaths sometimes seem likeable, too.* How many times had Craig lectured her with those admonitions? She was too trusting, he'd said. Too willing to believe in people.

Poor Craig. He had been an honest, dedicated cop. He should have gone to a big city and worked to retirement age solving complex homicides; he didn't deserve to be gunned down in a petty liquor store robbery in Cocoa, Florida. He'd talked about moving on to a bigger, urban department.

He might have made the move if he hadn't met her.
Forcing back the thought, Holly drew in a deep breath
and forced her attention to the present. The time had
come to handle the situation posed by the shelving assistant. But not here. It was too silent in this cavernous
building, too isolated, too intimate. And she was aware
enough of him as a man to need a little more noise and
the assurance of other people around when she confronted him. "I, uh, appreciate your staying late to finish the section," she said.

"You looked pretty busy with the display."

Holly rose. "I don't know about you, but I've had
enough of this place for one day." She looked directly
into his eyes. "Sometimes I stop at the café across the
street for a snack before heading home. Would you care
to join me?"

He didn't bother to hide his surprise. "Sure," he said.

THE CAFÉ, too far from the beach to draw in the tourist
crowd, catered mostly to downtown merchants and
office workers. The only customers in the place when
Holly and Craig entered were two men in business suits
with their ties loosened and their coats hanging over the
backs of their chairs.

Lawyers, Holly thought. The yellow legal pads on the
table in front of them confirmed her assumption. The
waitress, Gin, was sitting on one of the round stools at
the counter, reading a folded newspaper and nursing a
cup of coffee, when they came in. "How you folks doing this evening?" she greeted warmly. "You just sit
anywhere you like. I'll be right over with a menu."

Holly surveyed the room tentatively. The counter would be uncomfortable, the tables too exposed. "A booth?" she suggested.

He agreed, and a few minutes later, they were drinking milk and anticipating the imminent arrival of the grilled cheese sandwiches they'd ordered.

"Grilled cheese sandwiches are a comfort food for me," Holly said, avoiding the subject she'd deliberately brought him here to discuss.

"Comfort food?"

"Comfort food," she repeated. "Food that has soothing psychological associations. My mother always made grilled cheese sandwiches for my sister and me when we were tired or feeling bad, so we both associate them with being loved and cared for."

She'd never seen eyes quite like his before, so blue. So *intense*. She ventured a smile, which she hoped would put him at ease and asked, "What are your comfort foods?"

The loneliness she dreaded seeing flared for an instant before he tore his gaze from hers and stared blankly at the colorful dessert menu clipped to the chrome napkin holder. "I'm not sure I have any."

"It's intriguing, isn't it, the associations people make in their minds?"

His gaze came back to hers. "The human mind is a mysterious thing."

A tingle shivered up Holly's spine. *Mysterious*. She'd said "intriguing." Such a subtle difference—why did his choice of words make her feel so ill at ease?

After what seemed a very long interval of awkward silence, she asked, "Do you like working at the library?"

"It's been interesting seeing how everything is organized, and how much work it takes to keep it that way," he replied thoughtfully. "But sometimes it gets monotonous doing the same thing over and over."

"Like straightening picture books."

"Picture books and biographies and general fiction and nonfiction—" He paused, and changed inflection as he observed, "You must like children, to be a children's librarian."

"Yes," she said, smiling. "I do. I love children."

Gin brought their sandwiches and told them to signal her if they needed anything. For a few minutes, they ate in silence. Holly did not find the grilled cheese sandwich particularly comforting. She was too aware of the male presence on the seat opposite hers. Her legs were tense from hugging her own seat in an effort to keep her knees from brushing his beneath the narrow table.

"Children like you, too," he said.

Holly hadn't been expecting him to resume their conversation so abruptly. She met his gaze without actually responding to his observation.

"I've watched you with them," he said. "I've seen the way they respond to you. They hang on to every word when you read to them."

I've watched you with them. He'd inadvertently stumbled onto the problem she was here to discuss with him.

"Holly?"

Wrested from deep thought, she looked at him blankly.

"Are you . . . is everything okay? You seem—"

Holly drew in a lungful of air and exhaled slowly. "I have a confession to make."

He leaned against the back of the seat and crossed his arms over his waist. His eyebrow lifted slightly. Significantly. Too significantly. "A confession? This sounds interesting."

A blush heated Holly's cheeks. "I—" She swallowed. Her voice was stronger when she began again. "I had an ulterior motive in inviting you here."

A despicable grin slid over his face. Despicable, but beautiful. And sexy.

Too sexy.

"If you thought you'd soften me up with a grilled cheese sandwich and then take me home and have your way with me, I have to warn you that I'll probably offer very little resistance," he said.

"That's not—" At that moment Gin arrived at the table.

"Are you finished with those plates?" she asked.

In response to their nods, she picked up the plates. "You folks need anything else? A cup of coffee? A piece of pie? A refill on the milk?"

"I'll take another glass of milk," Craig said.

"Just a glass of water," Holly said.

"One H-two-O, one cow juice, coming up," Gin said, already on her way to the kitchen. She was back in less than a minute with their beverages. "Sure I can't interest you in some pie?"

They shook their heads in unison. "Bottoms up, then. Just give me a holler if you change your minds."

Silence dropped like a settling cobweb over the booth as she walked away, leaving them alone. Holly cleared her throat and shifted self-consciously, forgetting that his long legs were within touching distance until a chance collision of knees gave her a shocking reminder. "Excuse me," she said hoarsely, drawing away from the contact as quickly as possible.

"I believe we were discussing your plan to seduce me," he said.

"We were discussing no such thing," Holly said, regaining some of her composure. "That is *not* the reason I invited you here."

He released an aggrieved sigh. "Oh, gee. That's too bad."

"In fact, it's just the opposite."

"You want me to seduce you, instead?"

"I want you to quit staring at me!" she said, then took a steadying breath. He seemed not to notice the silence, which Holly found intolerable. "I don't want to make a big deal of this," she said with forced calm. "I decided to talk to you about it directly before mentioning it to anyone else, but—"

His smirky grin was gone, replaced by a somber expression.

"I've tried to tell you, without having to confront you like this," she said, "that the way you look at me makes me uncomfortable, but you haven't taken my hints."

His somber expression grew into a full frown.

"I have a right to do my work without feeling uncomfortable," she said.

After a long pause, he said, "I never intended to make you uncomfortable. You just . . . I told you . . . you look so familiar."

"That accounts for the first day you were on the job. Or the first time you asked if we'd ever met. This has been going on for two weeks, and it's getting worse instead of better. If staring at me is your way of trying to . . . *score*, then you're in for a big disappointment, because I'm not—"

"I'm not trying to score."

"Oh, right. With all the talk about my seducing you, or you—"

"I was teasing," he said.

"I wasn't amused."

"That much is obvious."

The atmosphere in the booth was charged with tension. Holly studied a drop of condensing water trail down the side of her glass.

"You didn't seriously think that I thought you brought me over here to seduce me?" he said.

Holly touched a drop of water near the top of the glass with her forefinger, then watched it split into two rivulets before raising her gaze to his face again. "It's not appropriate for you to be joking with me about a possible sexual liaison, and it's certainly not appropriate for you to stare at me when I'm trying to work."

"Appropriate?" He growled the word.

In the narrow booth, he suddenly seemed larger than life. And volatile. For once, Holly could not read his emotions. They were fogged by intensity. She wondered if she'd made a gross error in judgment by confronting him here instead of at the library when other people were around. She didn't know this man, didn't know what he was capable of, yet she'd provoked him.

Quickly, so quickly that she didn't have time to anticipate his movement, he reached across the table and grabbed her wrist. Holly gasped. Fighting back an instinctive urge to jerk away from him and run as fast as she could, she froze, staring at her wrist as though it were something separate from her body. When she finally moved, it was only to tilt her head back far enough to lock her gaze with his. Her breathing was ragged.

The seconds that followed seemed like hours. Then, as quickly as he'd grabbed her, he lifted both his hands with fingers spread. "I'm sorry. I—"

He dropped his hands to the table and closed his eyes. His chest vibrated with a wracking sigh. For a moment, he was so still that Holly wondered how he could be breathing.

When he opened his eyes again, the loneliness was there. And the intensity.

"Do you want to know why I stare at you?"

"I—" Holly couldn't complete the thought. She wasn't sure what he was asking.

He looked into her eyes. Again, time was distorted, seconds stretched into hours. "It's because you're the only person I've seen in this city who looks even remotely familiar to me."

"I don't understand," Holly said. "Did you just move here? Are you homesick?"

"I have no home," he said with a chilling softness. "No one I care about."

He'd been homeless, she thought. He'd been homeless and, somehow, he'd made it to Cocoa and gotten the job at the library. It tied up all the loose ends that had earned him the Mystery Man designation with Meryl and Sarah.

Overwhelmed by the force of his anguish, she covered his hand with hers. "If you need to talk about it, I'll listen."

A sympathetic ear was all she had to offer him; she hadn't any strength to share, no explanations for life's injustices. She'd used up all her strength accepting Craig's death, she'd gone through all the possible explanations without finding even one that could make sense of what had happened.

"Maybe I *should* talk about it," he said.

"Sometimes it helps," Holly said. *Sometimes it was the only thing that did.*

He was silent so long that she wondered if he'd changed his mind about confiding in her. When he finally spoke, his voice was uncommonly soft. "Five weeks ago, I woke up in Cocoa General Hospital without the slightest idea where I was, who I was or how I'd gotten there."

"Amnesia?" she asked incredulously.

"Retrograde amnesia," he said. "I don't remember anything before waking up in that hospital room."

"Nothing?"

"Not my name, not who I am, not where I came from. I don't remember reading *Make Way for Ducklings* or what my comfort foods are. I don't even remember whether I had a mother to feed me comfort foods."

Holly tried to absorb what he'd told her. She tried to imagine what it must be like to wake up without a past, without an identity. "Someone must know who you are. How did you get to the hospital? Someone must have brought you."

"I got there in an ambulance. The paramedics peeled me off a side street half a block from Highway A1-A. The driver who hit me said I came out of nowhere and ran right out in front of him. He braked, but there was no way he could stop in time. The witnesses—and there were several—all corroborated his story."

"You didn't have identification on you? A driver's license?"

His shoulders lifted slightly in a weary shrug. "A few dollar bills folded in the pocket of my T-shirt. Aside from that, I was in what the cops referred to as typical beach clothes—nylon shorts that double as a swimsuit, a Ron Jon's T-shirt. They said the shirt was new, that I'd probably bought it within a day or two of the accident."

Holly's fingers were curled around his hand now, not merely on top of it. "Surely someone reported you missing."

"If there's a human being on earth who cares about me or knows who I am, they haven't come forward. They put a story with my picture over the wire services, but..." The sentence faded into a sigh. "The theory is that I was here on vacation, and no one's missed me yet."

He paused, swallowed. When he spoke again, his voice was tauter than ever. "That theory gets weaker as time passes. People come to Florida for two weeks, not two months."

"This must be awful for you." She had both her hands across the table now, sandwiching his left hand between them.

He covered the outside hand with his right palm and curved his fingers around it, clinging to the clump of their clustered flesh. "It's hell. The unanswered questions—"

They passed a long moment in silence. Holly hoped that her presence comforted him. Finally, she asked, "How did you end up working at the library?"

"They assigned a social worker to help me. I went through the jobs offered at the employment office, and working in a library was the only one that appealed to me that didn't require a degree or related experience. My social worker pulled some strings with the county to get me hired."

He smiled unexpectedly. "And then I saw you and, for the first time, I thought I recognized someone or something from my past. I was so sure—"

He squeezed her hands. "You can understand why I stared, can't you? Even when you insisted that we'd never met. I still . . . no one else seems familiar."

His eyes were so filled with sadness that Holly's heart ached for him. "I wish I could tell you that I know you. I wish I could tell you who you are and help you re- member, but . . . if we'd met, I would remember."

"I believe you. I just . . . it's so disappointing. I keep thinking—hoping—that you'll jog a memory of some kind."

"I still could. Obviously I resemble someone you care about."

"But not necessarily someone who cares about me." His hands convulsed around hers. "God, what kind of monster does a man have to be that he can fall off the face of the earth and no one notices."

"It hasn't been all that long."

"Only an eternity," he said.

Holly wished for magic words, but she knew any- thing she said to encourage him would sound shallow and placating. Another silence ensued, heavier than the previous one.

"I have a friend in the police department," she said. "Maybe he could help."

"The police have done everything they can." He gave a short, bitter laugh. "They fingerprinted me. It's reassuring to know I'm not a criminal. At least not one who's ever been arrested. Unless, of course, the computers just missed the critical match."

"If a computer could miss a critical match, then a human being could miss a critical missing persons report, couldn't they? It wouldn't hurt to have someone double-checking."

"I'm not feeling very optimistic at this point. But, sure, let him check away. I can use all the help I can get. I'll give you the name of the officer assigned to the case." He paused thoughtfully, then peered deeply into her eyes. "I wish I could assure you that I have nothing to hide, but the questions.... God, if I just knew why I ran out in front of that car." He sighed. "Who am I kidding? I'd give an arm just to know my name."

"Craig Ford isn't your real name," she mused aloud.

"The car that hit me was a Ford," he said. "Some heritage, huh?"

"And Craig?" she said, choking on the name. "What made you choose Craig?"

"Once, in the hospital, I woke up kind of hazy from the painkillers and there was a really heated scene on the television. A man was whispering, 'Marlena, Marlena,' and the woman whispered back, 'Craig. Oh, Craig!' It sounded like a good, solid name. A man's name."

"Yes," Holly agreed. She'd always loved it, so rough and male, just like—

He laughed wryly. "Maybe I was hoping I'd get as lucky with women as the guy in the TV soap seemed to be."

"You probably don't have much trouble in that department," she said without thinking.

His eyebrow shot up with prurient interest. "Is that an objective opinion or a personal one?"

"Purely objective," she said. "You needn't be modest. You lost your memory, not your eyesight. Look in the mirror."

He tilted his head back until it rested against the high back of the booth. "Sometimes at night, I lay awake and wonder if the fact that I was thinking about 'getting lucky' means that I'm not married."

He could be married.

He could be a lot worse, she realized with a shiver. A criminal. A killer. A child molester. Even he didn't know.

So what are you doing holding hands with him in a public place? she asked herself.

As if he'd sensed the direction of her thoughts, he withdrew his right hand, and relaxed the fingers of his left. "I'm sorry I made you uncomfortable. I'll try not to stare at you anymore."

"I won't be as skittish now."

His grin came easily. "Then maybe I'll stare a little from time to time. Just because I like the view."

3

"YOU WOULDN'T HAPPEN to have a beer, would you?"

"Sorry, Josh. If I had known you were coming by—" Holly had called her fiancé's partner to ask him to see what he could find out about Craig Ford. He had told her he'd get back to her, but she hadn't expected him to show up on her doorstep, especially in the middle of a monsoonlike storm.

He shrugged. "Then I'll take anything that's wet."

Holly opened a soft drink for each of them and put a bowl of pretzels on the coffee table within Josh's reach. He stretched out as though he owned the place, his head and shoulders nestled into a trio of throw pillows, his long legs spread out with his sneakered feet hanging off the edge.

She settled into an armchair, drawing her legs up under her, as Josh reached for a pretzel. "This is about Craig Ford, isn't it? Did you find out something?"

Something significant enough to bring him out in the rain so he could tell her in person?

"I talked to Mick Scalisi, the officer assigned to the case. Your friend was brought into emergency as a John Doe, just like he said."

Holly didn't realize that she'd been harboring doubts about the extraordinary tale Craig had told her until she felt the surge of relief the verification brought. "Thank you for checking."

He washed down the pretzels with a generous mouthful of soda. "It was just a matter of finding Scalisi and asking a few questions."

"You didn't have to go out in this weather," she said. "You could have phoned."

"I haven't seen you in a while. I wanted to know how you're doing."

Holly smiled her gratitude. Josh Newmark was almost as protective of her as Craig had been, although she suspected his solicitude grew from an old-fashioned chauvinistic philosophy that women needed someone to take care of them. He and Craig had been partners, and he took that partnership as seriously as he would have a family bond. He felt duty-bound to watch over Craig's woman. He would have felt the same way no matter who Craig's woman had been.

"I'm getting along, taking one day at a time." She paused, then asked, "Do you think you can find out anything new about . . . my friend?" She couldn't call the shelving assistant Craig in front of Josh. The memory of the Craig they'd both cared about was still too vivid to both of them.

"Trust me, I intend to find out everything I can about your *friend*, Holly."

"I don't think I like the way you said that."

"So sue me."

"Don't be a horse's backside, Josh. He's just an acquaintance. There's nothing like that going on."

"Right. The first time I hear from you in three months, and it's to ask a favor for an *acquaintance*."

Holly was tempted to remind him that his phone had buttons, too, but she decided against it. After all, he *was* trying to help her.

"This guy's trouble," Josh said, trying her patience even more. "I can smell it."

"I thought you said his story checked out."

"Oh, it checks out. But it's a crappy story. It has more holes in it than a truckload of Swiss cheese."

Disappointment settled deep in Holly's chest. She didn't want to believe that Craig Ford was a con man, or that her judgment could be so flawed. "What kind of holes?"

"He's no ordinary John Doe," Josh said. "The guy is healthy, immaculately groomed, has an expensive haircut and quality clothes. Somebody ought to be missing him."

"If he was on vacation—"

"So how did he get here? And how did he get around? There are no rental cars unaccounted for, no abandoned cars found around that time."

"Not everyone drives. Maybe he took a taxi from the airport."

"Scalisi couldn't find a taxi driver who remembered him," Josh said. "The man's trying to disappear. He's trying to get lost and stay lost."

"Why would anyone want to do that?" Holly said.

Josh's laugh was ugly. "There you go again. Little Holly Sunshine. Everything is sunny and bright, and everyone is nice and happy. And no one has anything they'd like to run from."

"Don't you Little Holly Sunshine me, Josh! I've talked to this man. He's tormented."

"So he says. But his story is just a little too convenient."

"He was hit by a car!" she said.

"He ran into the path of a slow-moving vehicle on a side street," Josh said. "Without ID. It's too tidy. Scalisi's been suspicious from the first."

"Okay," Holly said with a sigh. "Suppose you're right. Suppose he's faking. What's his angle? What's he running from?"

"Who knows? Maybe he got in over his head and couldn't make the payments on his BMW. Maybe he lost a bundle in Vegas and has loan sharks on his heels. Maybe he screwed a politician's wife and the cuckolded husband is after him. Maybe he just got tired of the wife, the kiddies and the nine-to-five grind and decided to start over without the baggage. Maybe he neglected to make a sizable deposit of company funds. Who knows? So what does he do? He runs out in front of a car and wakes up with no memory. Bingo!"

"But his picture went out over the wire services."

"Maybe his best friend was hung over and didn't read the paper that day. Or his neighbor saw it and thought, 'Hey, that looks just like so-and-so.' Heck, maybe the little woman is even in on it, knowing once the heat dies down, they can live it up on the absconded money. For all you know, he could be phoning home twice a day from a pay phone on the corner."

Everything he said sounded feasible. But Holly had looked into Craig's blue eyes and seen the anguish in his troubled soul. "He's not faking," she said. "I can tell."

"You can tell," he said derisively. "That's rich. What's this—female intuition at work?"

"Don't be a jerk," she said. "I'm entitled to an opinion. I've talked to the man. You haven't even met him."

"Hmm," he said. "But I've seen his picture. He's a good-looking guy. I'm sure he can be very persuasive."

"You're not giving me much credit," Holly said. "I'm not the type to swoon over every handsome man I meet. Craig's looks—"

"That's another possibility. The man could have chosen any name he wanted. But he chose Craig, and then he went to work at the very library where you work. Don't you consider that a little convenient?"

"It's a coincidence!" Holly replied. "He chose the name because of a soap opera character."

"He could be trying to get to you."

"What possible motive would anyone have to try to get to me?"

"Aside from the obvious?" he asked.

"Men don't have to throw themselves in front of a car and pretend to have amnesia in order to meet me," Holly said. "Any man who wants to strike up an acquaintance with me can walk right into the library and say hello."

"Unless he wants you to think it's purely coincidental."

"Josh! Again, what reason would a man have to get close to me? Aside from the obvious, of course."

"Craig and I were working on some sensitive cases."

In Cocoa? "Oh, puh-leese. Who do you think is after me—the FBI? The Mafia? The KGB?"

"I'm going to do everything I can to find out who he is for you."

"You've misread the situation," Holly said, thinking that she'd made a mistake bringing Josh into it. "I asked for your help so *he* can find out who he is, not so I can."

Josh finished his soft drink and set the can on the coffee table. "You're the one who asked me for help, and you're the one I'm doing it for." He sat up, then propped his elbows on his knees and leaned forward. "Look, Holly, I don't know how close you've gotten to this John Doe—"

"I work with him, Josh. He's scarcely more than an acquaintance."

"Whatever," he said skeptically. "Just . . . be careful."

"Craig's been dead over a year," she said.

He shrugged. "No one expects you to go into eternal mourning. If you want to find a new man, find a new man. But find one with a name and a history you can check out. This guy's trouble, whether his story's true or not."

"I don't want a new man," Holly said softly. "I want Craig back. I still miss him. Every day."

"So do I."

They passed a moment of silence rife with memories of the person Craig had been and what he had meant to them. Finally, Holly smiled gently. "How's the rookie coming along?"

For the next hour, Josh entertained her with stories about the trials and travails of breaking in the young officer who'd become his partner shortly after Craig's death. "So there we were in the alley, our weapons drawn, and out walks this scruffy cat. Malone panics and fires off a round. He misses the cat, but hits the garbage can and the bullet ricochets and breaks the window in the back door of the store. Then the burglar alarm goes off and all hell breaks loose. Soon we're surrounded by cops and my partner is trying to explain why he fired at an unarmed cat. The next day, Malone opens his locker and this huge cat comes charging out. The poor guy almost had to change his shorts."

"It's good to hear that cop humor hasn't changed."

"Life goes on," Josh said with a resigned sigh.

"Yes, it does," Holly agreed. Life did go on. It went on and on. But it didn't necessarily get easier.

THE OPEN-AIR Beachside Club had a live band every Friday night. Holly, Meryl and Sarah went there together after work at least once a month. Tonight, Craig Ford was with them, thanks to an impromptu invitation from Meryl as they'd filed out of the library at closing time. The band was playing a plaintive ballad made famous by the Righteous Brothers.

Sarah closed her eyes and sighed. "Tom Cruise. *Top Gun.*"

"I love this song," Meryl said dreamily.

"It was made for dancing," Holly said.

"Absolutely," Meryl agreed, giving Craig a wink. "It's a shame to let a song like that go to waste. Too bad no one's asked you to dance, Holly."

"I can take a hint," Craig said, reaching for Holly's hand as he rose from his chair. "Would you care to dance, Miss Bennett?"

"Do you know how?" she asked as he led her to the floor.

"Your guess is as good as mine." He grinned. "I guess we're about to find out."

They turned to face each other. "What if you don't?" she asked.

"Then we'll fake it." He slid his right arm around her shoulders. "It doesn't look all that difficult."

"I guess you know how," she said after he guided her into a flawless box step.

"I wonder where I learned." Holly heard the sadness in his voice.

"My cousin taught me," she said. "She was two years older and knew everything there was to know about being cool, so she took pity on me and showed me the basics. I was going to the sixth-grade dance and I was petrified."

She laughed softly. "The only trouble was, only three boys in our class had the courage to get on the floor, and they only danced with the most popular girls. Everybody else just stood around feeling geeky."

"You were never geeky."

"Everybody's either geeky or cool in the sixth grade. I was geeky." Had he deliberately pulled her closer, or had she unconsciously snuggled into the seductive warmth of his embrace?

Maybe it was the song, with those mellow lyrics and lulling melody, that made her loath to pull back and put some space between them. Or maybe it was the compassion she felt for him. Maybe it was simply the wonder of being in a man's arms again. Whatever it was, she allowed herself to melt into that wonder and warmth, allowed her cheek to settle against the hard chest that offered strength and pleasure.

She closed her eyes and relaxed. Her breathing deepened. The music seemed to seep into her. The tempo. The melody. The emotion.

A sigh slid from within her, almost as if it had originated in her soul. His after-shave taunted her with its familiarity, until she recognized it as the same brand Craig had worn. Her Craig.

It came to her in a rush, a fresh, poignant reminder of what she'd lost. He'd never hold her like this again. She'd never feel his chest beneath her cheek, never have his arms around her, never again be able to lift her face to his and taste the desire in his kiss.

"Oh, Craig," she whimpered, not meaning to voice the words.

His sigh ruffled through her hair. "I've waited an eternity to have you next to me like this."

Magic sentiment, wrong voice. He had misinterpreted the meaning of her words. She lifted her cheek from his chest and pulled away.

His arm tightened around her shoulders, his hand squeezed hers. "Don't leave," he said. "Not when I've finally got you where you belong."

She didn't have the will to resist the lure of his embrace. The band was nearing the end of the song. Where was the harm in staying right where she was for another few minutes? It was a comfortable place.

"You're wearing after-shave," she said.

"I bought it yesterday. Do you approve of my choice?"

She didn't have a chance to answer, because as the band reached the crescendo, he spun her in circles and then dipped her backward from the waist on the final note.

Holly had no trouble following as he led her in the dramatic flourish. She had plenty of practice with that exact step. Craig—her Craig—had done exactly the same thing at the end of every song they danced to. Accustomed to the dip, she had relaxed so that she would be limber, but, recognizing the coincidence, she went rigid so suddenly that he almost dropped her.

"Holly?" He supported her as she came upright.

"What made you do that?" she asked.

His expression telegraphed surprise and he laughed nervously. "I don't know." The laughter faded, and a sigh followed. "I wish to God I did."

"I'm sorry." How could she have been so thoughtless? "You . . . surprised me."

"I'd never have guessed that," he said. "You were right with me."

"I used to know someone who did the same thing," she said. I used to *love* someone who did the same thing.

Their gazes locked and, just for an instant, the rest of the world fell away. Holly no longer heard the chatter of the diners, the clinking of cutlery against plates, the raucous laughter from the bar. She was aware only of his eyes, of the poignant emotions she saw there. She recognized and felt them so intensely, it seemed almost as if the two of them were linked in some mystical way, each a part of the other, capable of sharing thoughts and feelings.

The moment passed. The band launched into a wild rendition of "Great Balls of Fire."

"Do you want to try again?" he asked, tilting his head toward the center of the dance floor.

"You should ask Sarah or Meryl," she said.

"Of course," he said. "The only male. I forgot."

Holly nodded. She welcomed the chance to sit down and think about what had just happened. She had known getting over Craig's death would be difficult, but she hadn't expected to react the way she had the first time she was in another man's arms. If only he hadn't been wearing that particular after-shave. Of all the brands available, why did he have to select the very brand Craig had always worn? And then, to spin her that way... What was this affinity she had with him? Why did she *feel* it when she looked into his eyes?

"He sure has some moves," Sarah said, pulling Holly from her thoughts.

Holly didn't have to ask to whom Sarah was referring. Her friend's attention was riveted on Craig Ford, who was gyrating frenziedly with Meryl to the music.

"I guess he *does* know how to dance," Holly mused aloud.

"Knows how? He could audition for Chippendales if he took off his shirt."

She was right. He was attracting attention from females throughout the room.

"You two were certainly chummy," Sarah said.

"It was just the song," Holly said.

"Right!" Sarah said.

"It was," Holly insisted. She stared at the candle in the middle of the table. "I don't think I was quite ready to ... you know, relate."

"I think you were relating pretty well."

"Too well."

"Come on, Holly. Quit fighting it. Give it a chance."

I'm so confused! Holly wanted to say, but she wasn't ready to discuss her innermost feelings with anyone. She hadn't even told her friends about Craig's amnesia.

After another song, Craig escorted Meryl back to the table and asked Sarah to dance. As soon as they were gone, Holly and Meryl had a conversation remarkably similar to Holly's earlier exchange with Sarah. But Meryl didn't let Holly off as easy as Sarah had.

"Admit it," she said. "You're attracted to the man."

"He's attractive, but—"

"He's attractive, all right, but that isn't what I said. Attractive is an adjective. I used 'attracted.' It's a verb, which implies some action on your part."

Holly covered her face with her hands and groaned. "I don't want to be attracted to him. It's too complicated."

"Well, if you're *not* attracted to him, you're sure sending out some mixed signals. There wasn't room to slide a piece of paper between the two of you when you were dancing."

Holly lowered her hands. "I was thinking about Craig."

Meryl's forehead furrowed in concern. "Not the Craig you were dancing with, I take it."

Holly shook her head.

"You'll get past it," Meryl predicted. She turned her attention to the couples on the dance floor. After a long pause, she added, "If ever I've seen a man who could help a woman forget, it's our shelving assistant."

No! Holly wanted to scream. *He makes me remember, not forget!* But maybe that was part of the process, she reasoned. Maybe she had to remember before she could finally let go.

After three or four songs, Craig and Sarah returned to the table winded and calling for a fresh round of drinks. The conversation afterward was sparse as they simply enjoyed the clear night and the music. They were discussing the possibility of calling for their check when the band began playing another mellow song.

Craig covered Holly's hand. "I believe this is the one you've been saving for me."

Holly wanted to refuse, but Meryl and Sarah were both watching her expectantly, and Holly just didn't feel up to enduring their inevitable lectures if she turned him down. So she returned to the floor with Craig Ford.

Again, his right arm curved around her shoulders, and his left hand cradled her right. Once more, she nestled her cheek across that broad, hard chest and felt as though she'd finally reached a safe harbor.

"You didn't say whether you approved of my choice," he said as they swayed together.

"Approved?"

"Of the after-shave."

"Yes," she whispered. "I've always liked this brand. I used to know someone who wore it."

He folded her a little closer. "I wonder if I did."

His voice held the plaintive sadness that she'd seen so often in his eyes. His chest rose beneath her cheek as he drew a deep breath, and sank as he released it in a rush. "Why don't you know me?" he asked, then added desperately, "Why don't you know my name?"

His intensity scared her. "I . . ." Her voice trailed off. She couldn't be expected to remember meeting someone she'd never met. "I wish I could help you."

"Everything about you is familiar to me," he said. "The way you feel against me. The way your hair smells. The way you move."

"You want to believe that you know me," she said, lifting her head and putting some distance between them. "I look familiar, so you're clinging to that. It's only natural that you would. You don't have anything else to grasp at."

"I know what you would taste like if I kissed you."

"Do you think I wouldn't remember a man I'd kissed?"

His face was grave. "Put your cheek back on my chest, Holly. Where it belongs."

Trembling, she did as he instructed. It felt right—too right.

She closed her eyes. God help her, but it felt right.

The second the music ended and she righted herself from the backward dip, she ran to the table, where Meryl and Sarah were studying the check.

She was still trembling as she sat down. Craig was only steps behind her.

"We decided that since everyone had the same things, we'd just split it four ways. Is that agreeable?"

Holly and Craig indicated that it was. "What does it come to?" Craig said, taking out his wallet. Meryl told them.

Holly felt numb as she opened her purse. Why her? Why, of all people, did she have to be the one to look familiar to him?

"We've decided to take a walk on the beach before we leave," Sarah announced.

"It's such a beautiful night," Meryl chimed in.

Holly smelled a setup, but chose not to make an issue of their manipulation. She found the ocean soothing, a good place to think. As much as she resented their attempts to push her into a relationship, a walk along the water's edge might prove therapeutic.

As Holly suspected they would, not long after they reached the tide line, Meryl and Sarah dropped back, leaving her paired with Craig.

They didn't talk at first. Holly walked briskly, letting the breeze caress her face and the sound of the ocean wash over her frazzled nerves. Craig kept up with her easily. He seemed content to walk in silence, as though he was tuned in to her mood and was sharing it.

Holly wondered what was going through his mind. For a moment, she envied him the freedom from the kind of memories that haunted her, from the pain of remembering sweetness and knowing that it had been snatched from her forever. It might be easier to live without the memories of what she'd lost.

Unexpectedly, he spoke. "Tell me about him."

Holly didn't look at him. She couldn't, knowing that if she looked in his eyes, she'd feel that strange connection. "Who?"

"The man you used to dance with. The man who wore the after-shave I'm wearing."

Holly sighed. He had no right to hear the story, to ask it of her, but his voice was gentle and coaxing. Persuasive. "His name was Craig," she said softly.

He emitted a small gasp of surprise, and a moment of silence followed before he said, "He was important to you."

It wasn't so much a question as a speculative observation. Holly stopped and turned to face the water, which stretched as far as the eye could see before disappearing beyond the horizon. The moon glistened like liquid silver on the undulating surf. "He was everything to me," she said softly.

"You loved him."

"With all my heart. We were going to be married."

"What happened?"

Holly swallowed. "He died."

Behind her now, he put his hands on her shoulders. She didn't question the liberty he took in touching her. His being there seemed too right.

"Can you talk about it?"

"He was a cop. He answered a routine call and then...he was gone." So few words! His life snuffed out, her life inexorably changed, their future destroyed, all summarized in a matter of sentences.

His arms slid around her, enfolding her. The familiar scent he was wearing blended with the briny breeze coming off the ocean, and for a moment—

Oh, Craig—why did you have to die? She relaxed against the strength and solidity of the man holding her. How long they stood there, with the ocean slapping the packed sand just inches from their feet, she wasn't sure. Nor did she care. She had done so much of her grieving alone, and had had so little human consolation once the funeral was over and everyone had gone back to their busy lives. She'd purposely kept her grieving private, not wanting to burden anyone else with the desolation that plagued her. But she was tired of being strong, of holding up, of pretending. It was a relief to lean on someone else for a change.

Gradually, the texture of the embrace changed. Comfort segued into awareness, and the contact took on a sensual quality. The emptiness Craig's death had left inside Holly suddenly became unbearable. She had lived with the loneliness one day too long, and she was desperate for a man's touch, for the affirmation that she was desirable, for the confirmation that she was still capable of feeling desire.

Without a word, she turned in his arms and tilted her head back. Without a word, he lowered his lips to hers and claimed her kiss.

4

THE FIVE MILES from the beach to the Victorian house two blocks from the library had never been longer. Holly didn't know why she was surprised that Craig Ford had wound up in her car. She'd known Meryl and Sarah were setting her up the moment Meryl had casually invited Craig to join them for dinner. She should have anticipated the argument that, since she was the only one who would be passing the library on her way home, it made sense that she should be the one to take Craig home.

So there they were—side by side in the front seat of her compact car, she and Craig Ford. And between them, sat The Kiss.

For half of the endless trip, seven minutes that seemed more like a week, they ignored each other so vehemently that neither of them dared to speak. Holly had no idea what he was thinking, but from his demeanor, she suspected that he was as shaken as she by what had happened between them.

The Kiss had been none of the things a first kiss was supposed to be. Not short. Not sweet. Not tentative. It had been a kiss of lovers, hot, urgent and demanding. And it had gone on forever, or threatened to, titillating, inflaming, exciting.

They'd parted shocked and trembling, stunned by the swiftness with which their passions had been aroused. Without saying a word, he'd taken her hand in his. They'd walked farther along the beach, letting the sea breeze cool them before they turned around to walk in the opposite direction, knowing they'd soon encounter Meryl and Sarah.

Holly stopped for a traffic signal and stared through the windshield at the glistening red orb of light. *Just a few more minutes, and then she could go home to her small apartment, to the furniture she selected for comfort, to the cat who would saunter over to demand affection.*

Craig spoke unexpectedly. "I knew it would be that way."

Holly twisted her head to look at him.

"I told you when we were dancing that I knew what it would be like to kiss you," he continued intently. His face was a mask of anguish and frustration. "If we don't know each other, how do I know you so well? How could we be that familiar to each other? *Why don't you know my name, Holly?*"

His belligerent, challenging tone sent goose bumps up her spine. What did she know about him, really? Indeed, what did he even know about himself and what he was capable of?

"Are you accusing me of deceiving you?" she asked woodenly.

He didn't answer. The silence grew thick and oppressive.

"The light's green," he said at last. Holly stepped on the gas pedal. "I wouldn't withhold that kind of information from you," she said after a pause, not looking at him. "I'm not capable of such cruelty."

She heard him exhale wearily before he said, "I...it's just so damned frustrating. How can I *know* you if I don't know you? And why it is that you're the only person who seems familiar to me?"

"You're not remembering me," she said. "You can't be. You're remembering someone who looks like me."

"Looks wouldn't account for what happened between us tonight. That was chemistry, person-to-person."

Holly pondered the point a moment. "Doesn't it make sense that if you were attracted to a certain type of woman—a certain physical type, I mean—that you'd be attracted to the same type now? If I resemble someone you love, then you may be reacting physically to me the way you'd react to her."

"No," he said. "It's you."

She found his conviction unnerving.

She waited until they had reached his house before speaking again. After pulling up to the curb, she turned to look at him. "You're reaching," she said. "I'm the only thing you have to cling to, and this . . . *feeling* you have that you know me has taken on more importance than it deserves."

His jaw was clenched, his mouth hard. In an eruption of emotion, he brought the pad of his hand down on the dashboard. "Damn it, who am I? And who the hell do you remind me of?"

"If I could answer those questions for you, I would," Holly said quietly.

He looked at her a long moment, then turned away. "I'm sorry, Holly. I keep trying to make you a part of this, when—"

A lengthy sigh vibrated through him. Holly had never seen a person appear more alone. "You need a friend," she said.

He looked at her and smiled sadly. "I wonder if I have any."

She returned the smile. "You have one sitting right here, if you want one."

"Want one?" he said in a rush. "God, Holly—"

He put his arm across the seat and leaned toward her, cradling her cheek with his right hand. His intentions were unmistakable. Holly's breath caught. She twisted her head away from his hand and swallowed. "That's not part of the friendship package."

He withdrew his hand, but left his arm behind her.

"It wouldn't be ... *healthy* for either of us," she said. "I'm ... I thought I was ready, but tonight ... at the beach ... I realized that I still have a lot of sorting out to do. And you—"

"I have no right to ask, not when I don't know—"

Her heart went out to him; he was so miserable. "Can we be friends?" she asked.

"I would like that."

"I'll see you tomorrow, then."

He nodded. "Thanks for the ride."

She watched him let himself into the house before driving away.

The phone was ringing when she arrived home a few minutes later. Assuming it was either Meryl or Sarah wanting to talk about what had happened on the beach, she stood next to the answering machine and waited for the caller to leave a message.

Meryl's voice came over the speaker. "Holly—give me a call so we can *talk*."

Her emphasis on the word *talk* confirmed what the subject of their conversation would be, so Holly let her hang up without picking up the phone. She wasn't ready to "talk" about what had happened on the beach. She hadn't sorted it out in her own mind yet.

She had been vulnerable. It had been her first physical contact with a man since Craig's death. But that didn't fully account for her explosive reaction to Craig Ford. The chemistry between them was strong, as strong as the emotional chemistry that had linked her to him the first time she'd looked closely into his eyes. And his insistence that he knew her was unsettling. He seemed so sure, so positive. He was as convinced that they had met as she was that they had not. Her strong reaction to his touch wasn't doing anything to shake his confidence in that conviction.

The only thing clear to her at this point was that she was going to have to avoid getting into situations where her hormones could feed his delusion that he knew her.

"YOU WON'T BELIEVE why I'm late," Holly said, locking the drawer on the cabinet where the librarians kept their purses while on duty.

"A full five minutes," Sarah teased. "We were getting ready to send out the militia to hunt for you."

"I wish you had," Holly said. "I could have used some help. I was chasing a skink."

"A skink!"

"Yes. I was just finishing my cereal, when I heard something rustle the blind on the living room window. I looked over just in time to see a huge skink leap from the sill into the middle of the floor."

"How huge?"

"As big around as my pinkie and half a foot long, plus tail."

Craig, who'd been straightening reference books, stood up. "What's a skink?"

"You're not from Florida, are you?" Sarah asked.

Holly saw the pain the question inflicted skitter across his face before he replied, "Apparently not."

"Well, sooner or later, anybody who lives in Florida encounters a skink."

"Want to give me a hint what they look like so I'll know when I've seen one?" he suggested.

"It's a lizard," Holly said.

"But it looks more like a snake with legs," Sarah said with a shiver. "It's shiny and jet black. Or so blue it looks black."

"Are they poisonous?"

"They don't bite, but if a cat or dog eats one, it can make them really sick or even kill them," Holly answered. "That's why I had to catch the one in my house before Buttercup found it."

"Buttercup?" Craig asked.

"Holly's cat," Sarah said, then turned to Holly. "How did you catch it?"

"I didn't. I trapped it under a trash can. I'm going to have to worry about getting it outside when I get home tonight."

"*Eeeeeeeee,*" Sarah said, shivering again.

"Exciting Saturday night, huh?" Holly said drolly. "Actually, I'm hoping that Mrs. Grayson is baby-sitting her grandson tonight so I can get him to catch it. He loves creepy, crawly things. Otherwise, I'll just have to slide a cookie sheet under the can and carry the little squirmy little devil out myself, garbage can and all."

"That sounds like a lot of trouble," Craig observed. "Why not just pick it up?"

"Pick it up?" both women asked in unison as though he'd suggested they swallow it alive.

"I couldn't *touch* it," Holly said.

Craig chuckled.

"They move like lightning," Holly said defensively. "I probably couldn't even catch it, and if I did, they're too squiggly to hold on to."

"Squiggly?" he asked, disbelieving.

"They *are* squiggly," Sarah assured him.

"Oh, I'm sure they are," Craig said, obviously amused.

"I just don't touch lizards," Holly said, bristling.

"It's a girl thing," Sarah explained.

Craig rolled his eyes. "I'm going back to work."

Holly forgot all about the lizard as she dealt with the Saturday crowd in the children's section.

As closing time approached, the area remained busy, and Holly resigned herself to staying late to put the section in order. Once again, Craig showed up to help. They straightened the picture-book shelves from opposite ends, just as they had the first time he'd worked in the reading corral. They reached the base of the U at the same time and exchanged smiles.

"So," he said, "other than evicting a skink, do you have a big Saturday night planned?"

"Not a lot," Holly admitted. "There's a movie I've been wanting to see on cable."

Craig paused thoughtfully. "I could try to catch your skink for you."

Holly considered the offer, which he'd presented with an almost heartrending earnestness. His hope was almost palpable. He was lonely, she realized. It was Saturday night, and he had no one to spend it with.

Nor had she.

"Sure," she said. "Why not? You can watch the movie with me."

He smiled endearingly. "I'd like that."

THE OVERTURNED TRASH CAN, weighted down with a heavy book, was quite conspicuous as they entered her apartment a half hour later. "So that's where the little guy is," Craig said.

"Hopefully," Holly said. "If the book was heavy enough to keep him from slithering underneath the rim."

Unexpectedly, there was a hard thunk on the far side of the closed door at the end of the hall, followed by an impatient howl. "That's Buttercup," Holly said. "She must have heard us come in. I put her in the bedroom so she wouldn't hear the scratching inside the can and knock it over. She's probably going stir-crazy. She can't stand closed doors. I'd better go give her some attention and calm her down. Just . . . make yourself at home."

She gave Buttercup a thorough rubdown, then took advantage of the private moments in her bedroom to change into comfortable clothes, a one-size-fits-all T-shirt over stretch leggings and a pair of socklike slippers. She removed the barrette at her nape and brushed her hair, leaving it free around her shoulders.

Shooing Buttercup away from the door, she left the bedroom to rejoin Craig. Buttercup was already butting the door, protesting being confined again by the time she reached the living room, where Craig was sitting on the couch. He stood as she approached, in an automatic reflex that bespoke etiquette training in his early years. She wondered if he realized that might be a clue to his identity, or, at least, to the nature of his upbringing, but chose not to bring up the subject just then.

He was smiling at her, and the glint in his eyes was clearly one of frank approval. She was both pleased and uneasy. Being admired by a man, especially one as attractive as Craig Ford, was flattering. But without realizing how it might seem to him, she had, literally, changed into something more comfortable and let her hair down. And the way he was looking at her made her fear that she had given him the erroneous impression that she had selected her attire and hairstyle with seduction, instead of comfort, in mind.

She decided to tackle the potential misunderstanding head-on. "I hope you don't mind my changing into my grubbies," she said, choosing the most unromantic word she could think of. "I thought my skirt might be a bit formal for skink chasing."

Craig had never seen a woman who looked less grubby. Or less like a librarian. She looked...delicious. He shrugged benignly. "If I had any grubbies, I'd have changed into them, too."

"That's right," she said as comprehension dawned. "You wouldn't have any clothes, would you?"

"The shorts and T-shirt I was wearing when I had the accident were ruined. The social worker found some clothes for me to work in, but not much else," he told her. "She gave me a list of local thrift shops, but I haven't gone to any yet." He paused. "I like your hair that way."

Light brown, it framed her face in loose waves. She combed her hand through it self-consciously, tucking the front strands behind her ear on one side. "The barrette gives me a headache if I keep my hair pulled back too long."

Another impatient thunk from the bedroom drew Craig's attention. "How big is that cat, anyway?"

"She's not all that big. I think she takes a flying leap at the door."

"We'd better evict that skink before Buttercup hurts herself," he said chuckling.

"I'll get the broom," Holly said, spinning on her heel and exiting the room.

"The broom?"

"In case it makes a dash for it," Holly called from the kitchen. She returned, armed for combat. The way she was wielding the broom, bristle-end up, like a cudgel, she could have defended her virtue against plundering Viking hordes.

"Are you sure you don't want a more substantial weapon?" Craig asked, still smiling. "A cannon, perhaps? Or an Uzi?"

She responded with a pout of irritation that sent his blood pressure soaring. For a chance to taste those pouty lips again, he'd face a fire-breathing dragon. Putting those thoughts aside, he knelt next to the wicker trash can, removed the book and set it aside. "Ready?"

Holly gave a little nod and tensed, prepared to spring into action.

Gingerly, he tilted up the rim a fraction of an inch with his left hand, his right poised to capture any critter that came scurrying out. Nothing happened. He tipped it back some more. The skink was perched on the wall of the can, near the bottom. It was a fierce-looking creature, yet strangely beautiful, a shade of blue so deep it appeared black and iridescent, larger than the lizards that inhabited the flower beds around the Victorian house where he lived.

The skink demonstrated no inclination to move. Petrified with fear at being confronted by human beings, Craig reasoned, heaving a sigh of relief. "Piece of cake," he said, curving his hands around the trash can and lifting it ever so gradually as he rose. "We just take this outside and—"

A flying leap took the skink from one side of the can to the other, and then, with lightning speed, the creature was over the top and sailing to the floor. It hit the carpet running. A well-placed thack of the broom diverted it sideways. Craig darted into the skink's new path and, lunging to the floor, attempted to trap it in his hands. It eluded him by the smallest margin and raced on.

Again, Holly forestalled it with the broom, forcing it to detour again, surprising Craig with an acrobatic leap over his arm en route.

"This is war!" Craig growled, scrambling after the fleeing reptile. This time, it was the wall that forced a detour. Craig continued to pursue the runaway skink, glancing at Holly to see if she was ready to head it off again. She was standing with the broom back in strike position. But when the skink scurried past her, she didn't move. Craig redoubled his efforts to catch the lizard, rounding the corner and entering the hall-way. Holly didn't follow. She was too stunned. *"This is war!"* One of Craig's favorite expressions. *Her* Craig's. Spoken with the same inflection, the same fervor, under the same type of circumstances Craig would have said it.

Her cheeks were burning, yet she felt hollow and cold inside. Coincidence, she told herself. It was coincidence, pure and simple—what else could it be? It was slang, jargon, in wide use by a lot of people around Craig's age.

How long she stood there, feeling empty, remembering Craig, missing him with a fresh sharpness of grief, she could not have said.

"I caught him!" The voice of Craig the shelving assistant, quite different from that of the Craig to whom she'd been engaged, drew her out of her reverie. He stepped out of the bathroom with his hands clasped together and his eyes wide open in urgency. "Open the door!"

She did as he instructed and watched him trot, arms extended, to the hedge along the sidewalk that ran beside the apartment building, where he eased his hands apart, then dusted them together as if to say, "Mission accomplished." Grinning from ear to ear, he strolled back to her apartment. "You can let your cat out now."

He followed her as far as the bathroom. "I'm going to wash my hands, if you don't mind."

"Mind?" Holly said. "I insist!"

She opened the bedroom door for Buttercup, then proceeded to the kitchen. They'd stopped at the supermarket deli for cold cuts on the way to her apartment, and she opened the wrappers and arranged the meats and cheeses on a platter. Buttercup circled her feet, rubbing against her ankles and meowing for handouts. Holly gave the cat a sliver of ham, then looked up as Craig approached from the hallway.

"Can I help?" he offered.

"There's not that much to do. But, here—" She took plates from the cabinet and flatware from the drawer. "You can set the table in the dining room."

"Is the wine chilling?" he asked from the breakfast nook.

The wine. She'd forgotten about the wine. She'd insisted on paying for the cold cuts, since they were going to dine in her home, so he'd countered by selecting a bottle of wine. "No," she admitted, embarrassed. "I'll stick it in the freezer. It won't take long."

"Wine in the freezer?" he asked as though she'd suggested they put ketchup on prime rib. "Don't you have an ice bucket?"

"No. I—" Craig's aunt and uncle had sent them an ice bucket for a wedding present. Like all the other gifts, she'd returned it when Craig died. "I usually make do with a bowl." She rummaged in the cabinet until she found one the right size, then filled it with ice cubes.

Craig finessed the bottle into the ice and, pressing the neck between his palm, gave it a gentle spin. Later, after pronouncing it adequately chilled, he removed the cork expertly, despite the primitiveness of the corkscrew with which Holly had supplied him.

"What shall we toast?" Holly asked, lifting her goblet.

"Life without skinks?" he suggested.

Holly touched her glass to his. "To life without skinks—thanks to your help." He nodded and they both sipped. "This wine is delicious," Holly said.

"It's German. A Mosel. *Mit pradikat.*"

"I don't know what you're talking about," Holly confessed. "You've probably surmised that I'm not much of a wine connoisseur."

"*Mit pradikat* is the highest grade of German wine. There's *tablewein*, for everyday use, and *qualitat*, and *qualitat mit pradikat*. Sort of good, better and best."

Holly set her goblet down and stared at him a moment. "Is this something you've learned since your accident?"

The question stunned him a moment. "No," he said. "No. I wonder—" Without warning, he brought his fist down on the table. "Damn it!"

"Craig," she said softly, consolingly.

Frustration torturing his features, he said, "Why would I remember what *mit pradikat* means, when I can't recall my own name?"

She laid her hand on his arm. "This could be a very positive sign. The fact that you know how to pick out a good wine says something about you, about your lifestyle."

"Maybe the nurse was right," he said bitterly.

"What nurse?"

"The one I overheard in the hospital. The one who said that with my looks, I'd probably turn out to be a gigolo."

"That's ridiculous!"

"Why?"

"Because," Holly replied, but any real reason eluded her.

"Because it would be nicer if I turned out to be an attorney or a brain surgeon?"

"You're not a gigolo," Holly insisted.

His smile was bittersweet. "Thanks for the vote of confidence. Unfortunately, I seem to have a great familiarity with wine, and no particular urge to to address a jury."

"Maybe you're a chef. Or a waiter. Or maybe you just like wine. A lot of people do. It's a social asset."

"Let's talk about something else," he said curtly.

"All right," she said, smiling as she took her hand from his arm. "What shall we talk about?"

Studying her face intently, he grinned sensually, then said, "You."

"I'm a small-town librarian. What's to talk about?"

"Why?"

"Why what?" She piled ham, turkey and Swiss cheese on a piece of rye bread.

"Why did you become a librarian?"

"Well, I was going to be a supermodel and travel to exotic ports, but they make you stand in the most awkward positions when you're doing the *Sports Illustrated* swimsuit spread—"

"Seriously," he said.

"You saw right through the supermodel story, huh?"

"You're too . . . genuine to be a supermodel."

Holly grinned. "You aren't a gigolo. You're a diplomat."

"You're evading the question," he countered.

"There's nothing dramatic about it," she said. "I've always loved books, I've always loved libraries. So I became a librarian. And I've always loved the ocean, so I applied for jobs in coastal cities. Cocoa had an opening for a children's librarian, and I've always loved children, so . . ."

"It sounds as though you've found the perfect job."

"I'll never get rich, but yes, it's a great job. I get to be creative, and there's a lot of satisfaction in introducing children to books in an era of compact disks and video recorders."

"You're getting a little competition from high-tech these days."

"Not just a little. A lot. Now even the media that once relied on reading are presented via voice, with moving pictures. Like the encyclopedias on compact disk. It's wonderful that children can look up 'opera' and actually see and hear a performance on a computer screen, but we can't let future generations rely entirely on computers. They must learn to read for themselves, as well. And what better way can we get them to do that than to introduce them to the sheer pleasure and excitement of books?"

She stopped and smiled sheepishly. "I get a little carried away sometimes."

"You're passionate about your work," he said. "That's nothing to be embarrassed about."

"I'm dedicated," she said. "I don't know about passionate."

"I have a feeling you're a very passionate person," he said, his gaze fixing on her face. "About many things."

Holly might have argued with him if the way he was looking at her hadn't had such a profound effect on her senses. They finished their meal in relative silence, then cleared the table and put away the leftovers before refilling their glasses and carrying them to the living room.

"I've heard the movie coming on is hysterically funny," Holly said, as she sat down and picked up the remote control. She clicked to the proper channel, then hit the mute button until it was time for the movie to start.

"I hope so," Craig said. "I could use a few laughs."

"I kept thinking I'd go see it when it got to the bargain cinema, but I never got around—"

"Ho-lee—" Buttercup had made a flying leap into Craig's lap, and he was struggling to keep his glass upright.

Holly giggled. "I should have warned you when you first sat down. Buttercup adores men. She's probably yours for as long as you sit there, unless you want me to put her back in the bedroom."

Craig put his glass on the coffee table and gave the cat's head a tentative pat. "Don't lock her up. I don't mind her sitting on my lap. She just surprised me."

Within seconds, the cat was sprawled across his thighs on her back, purring like a well-tuned engine while he rubbed her neck.

"She's such a hussy!" Holly said.

"She just likes comfort," he said, grinning at the cat's blatant display of ecstasy. "I should have this effect on women!"

"What makes you think you don't?" She'd said it without thinking.

"If I did," he said, grinning mischievously, "would you be sitting all the way over there?"

"If you didn't," Holly countered, "maybe I wouldn't have to sit all the way over here. I could sit on the couch and watch television without getting a crick in my neck." She was flirting. And it felt good....

Stretching his arm to pat the cushion on the opposite end of the couch, he said, "Come on over." His grin slid into a sensual smile. "I promise not to make you purr unless you fling yourself across my lap."

"I think I can resist flinging myself long enough to watch a movie," she said, moving to the couch.

Actually, she wasn't all that sure—either that she could resist his allure or that she wanted to. The only thing she was sure of was that she *should*.

5

HOLLY WAS BEING RECKLESS and she liked it. The coquette in her had been dormant too long not to glory in the danger of flirting, the thrill of teasing and testing a mutual attraction. She'd been too long without a man's attention and touch.

She was not actually touching him, of course. Well over two feet of sofa cushion stretched between them once she sank into her end of the couch. At first, it seemed far too insignificant a space. But as the movie played on, and they laughed together and shared observations about the quirky characters and outlandish plot twists, that gap seemed to grow frustratingly wider. It became imposing. And then, magically, it began to shrink.

A subtle slide of a knee, a casual drop of the hand, an almost imperceptible shift of position. Holly wasn't aware that she'd moved any more than she was that he had, but, suddenly, feet had dwindled to mere inches. She could feel the warmth emanating from him, smell the familiar after-shave he wore, hear Buttercup's soft purr and occasional sigh as she slept. Reflexively, Holly reached out to massage the cat's ears, accidentally brushing the side of her hand against Craig's. Their gazes met as sexual awareness shot between them like an electrical spark.

The moment should have been awkward, but it wasn't. They simply acknowledged what had happened, then exchanged knowing smiles before returning their attention to the movie.

How could she be so comfortable with him? she wondered. How could they be so comfortable with each other? They were like lovers who'd been together a long time, tuned in to the nuances of each other's mood.

The movie ended, and neither of them moved until the copyright notice trailed the last credits across the screen. "Wacky movie," Craig said.

"Yes," Holly agreed. "It was just the way everyone described it, kind of—"

"Hard to describe."

"Yes. Zany and a little off-the-wall." Holly picked up the remote control and hit the mute button as the promos for coming presentations blared through the television speakers. "I don't think I'd care to see a boxing match. How about you?"

Craig shook his head. Holly knew the wise thing to do would be to thank him again for capturing the skink and deliver him to his door, but she was loath for the evening to end, loath to give up the companionship he offered. How long had it been since she'd enjoyed a Saturday night?

"I could take you home," she said, "but it's still early. I have a video of *Arsenic and Old Lace*. It's my favorite movie of all time. I watch it a couple of times a year. If you'd like to stay..."

"I'd love to stay," he said, unable to hide his delight.

"Good," Holly said, pretending she hadn't known he would accept the invitation. She moved forward on the couch, ready to stand. "I'll stick some popcorn in the microwave."

A few minutes later, she was pouring the freshly popped corn into a bowl, when Buttercup let out a guttural shriek of aggression. Grinning, Holly shook her head. Craig and Buttercup were at it again. They always—

A shiver crept up her spine. Craig was the only person who'd ever made Buttercup growl that way. Not the Craig sitting on her sofa, but the Craig she'd planned to marry. Abandoning the popcorn, she dashed to the living room. Then, feeling like a fool, she watched Craig Ford fencing with her cat, forefinger to front paws. Buttercup growled ferociously and parried with her paw. "Why are you playing with her like that?" Holly asked sharply.

Surprised, Craig looked up. "She rolled on her back and I was rubbing her chest and suddenly she started swatting at my hand. She seems to enjoy it. I figured you played with her like this all the time."

"No," Holly said, forcing herself to sound calm. "It's . . . she only plays that game with men."

Craig chuckled as Buttercup released another deep-throated growl. "Ferocious beast! She doesn't even have her claws out." He paused for a moment, then said, "That popcorn smells good."

"It's ready. I'll get it," Holly said. She returned to the kitchen and reached for the bowl, then dropped her hands on the cabinet on either side of it. Bowing her head, she closed her eyes and drew in a deep breath. For a few glorious seconds, she'd forgotten that her Craig was dead; then, when she'd seen Craig Ford playing with Buttercup the way only her Craig ever had, when she'd heard Buttercup's growls . . .

It was the little things, the tiny, insignificant little things you never really paid any attention to, that caught you at the most unexpected moment and turned you inside out. Holly released a ragged sigh, squared her shoulders, picked up the bowl of popcorn and forged onward to the living room, grabbing the bottle of wine along the way.

"I've never had wine with popcorn," she said after putting the video into the VCR and sinking onto the sofa beside him. "I think I'm going to like it."

"What's this movie about, anyway?" Craig asked as the copyright-infringement warning flashed on the screen.

"Murder and insanity," Holly answered, scooping up a handful of popcorn. "It's hysterical."

"Oh, sure," he said. "Murder and insanity are always amusing."

"Just wait," she said. "You'll be rolling on the floor."

Craig thought that he wouldn't mind rolling around on the floor a bit if Holly was rolling around with him. "One can always hope," he muttered.

"It's starting," Holly said, rolling her shoulders against the back cushions of the couch as she settled in. "Watch carefully. Everything builds as the story goes along."

"Uh-huh," he said absently. The leading man, Mortimer Brewster, author of *The Bachelor's Bible*, had dragged the leading lady out of the marriage-license line and was explaining that he couldn't marry her. The leading lady was holding up well, meeting the news with stoic acceptance and a look that would have melted even the most cynical heart.

"He's a goner. She's giving him the treatment," he said.

"She's just looking at him," Holly said innocently.

Craig sniffed disdainfully. "No woman ever 'just looks' at a man. See that quiver in her chin. Look at her eyes. He's going to kiss her any second now. See! Told you he was a goner."

"Oh, yeah," Holly said. "You can tell he's suffering."

"He's on his way back to the marriage-license line," he observed.

"All because of a look."

"Never underestimate the power of a look."

He waited until she dipped her hand into the popcorn bowl and dipped his hand in, too. The moment their fingers touched, she turned to face him with that wide-eyed expression of surprise that always formed on her features when the most innocent contact sparked an electric reaction between them.

"Sorry," he said, pretending he had not intentionally orchestrated the encounter.

She smiled forgiveness and turned her attention back to the movie. Craig took advantage of her preoccupation to study her profile, fascinated by the soft curve of her cheek, intrigued by the way her nose tilted just the tiniest bit at the tip, giving her a kitten cuteness, which should have been at odds with her sexiness instead of enhancing it. She was so sweet, he wanted to lick her like a lollipop until she melted.

He managed to keep up with the story line of the movie despite the distracting way her shirt draped over her breasts, molding their roundness with sufficient detail to make a man dizzy for want of filling his hands with them. He held out until the charming, aged Brewster sisters were trying to serve up another portion of lethal elderberry wine before he shifted restlessly and stretched his arm along the back of the sofa— behind Holly's head.

The movie was every bit as funny as Holly had told him it would be. Cary Grant, playing drama critic Mortimer Brewster, juggled his aunts' homicidal antics, his sadistic Frankensteinian brother and bodies competing for space in the window seat.

Craig and Holly grinned, chuckled and bellylaughed. They relaxed, gravitating ever nearer to each other. Holly's left shoulder nestled against his ribs. His hand dropped to her right shoulder, cradling and caressing. Her hair was silky under his chin and smelled lightly of flowers. He thought that if he didn't kiss her soon, he would expire from sheer anticipation.

His opportunity came at long last near the end of the movie as Mortimer drew his new bride into his arms and kissed her to keep her quiet about the bodies in the basement. "Now *there's* a man who knows how to handle a woman," he said.

Holly answered with a sigh, "Cary Grant always knew."

"Think I'll borrow his technique," he said, closing his arms around her.

Holly hadn't the will to resist as his mouth covered hers, then became greedy as her lips softened and yielded. He was warm, strong, male; gentle but persuasive. She cradled his cheek in her palms then slid her hands higher, threading her fingers into his hair as the kiss deepened. He tore his mouth from hers to drag damp kisses along her jaw en route to her neck. A sensuous whimper of arousal escaped her as his hot, questing lips explored soft, sensitive skin. His hands were splayed across her back, supporting her, holding her close.

Holly lowered her hands to his shoulders and slid her arms around him, leaning across his lap, to the chagrin of Buttercup, who leaped away with a mewl of protest and cast them a disgruntled look over her shoulder on the way out of the room. "We've hurt her feelings," Holly said breathlessly.

"She'll get over it," Craig returned in a rasp. His mouth found hers again. He seemed to be touching her everywhere, and every place he touched her throbbed with pleasure.

"Is this when we get to roll on the floor?" Craig asked hopefully.

Holly groaned her regret and drew her hand forward to cradle his cheek. She gazed into his eyes. "This is when I take you home."

His groan was deeper, more prolonged and more filled with regret than hers had been. He stroked her hair away from her face. "That girl in the movie was an amateur compared to you. Your eyes are doing me in."

"I think it's the other way around," she said dreamily. "Your eyes—" Smiling gently, she traced each of his eyelids with her forefinger. "They're so blue."

His smile was bittersweet frustration. "You're torturing me."

She craned her neck to kiss him briefly on the lips. "Time to go, bucko!"

OUTSIDE, the night was unnaturally black, the sky starless and overcast. The air held the heavy stillness of impending rain. After commenting on the chances of a storm, they passed the short trip to his house in comfortable silence that extended a minute or so past the time that Holly parked at the curb and turned off the engine. A distant street lamp provided the only light inside the car.

"Thank you for catching my skink," Holly said finally. Hearing a whisper of movement, she turned her head and found Craig looking at her.

He grinned. "Thank you for the movies."

Another silence ensued before Holly said, haltingly, "You were a good sport about—"

He lifted his shoulders in a halfhearted shrug. "You made the ground rules clear the last time you brought me home."

"Some men might have pressed their advantage."

"Every minute I spend with you is special, Holly. I wouldn't do anything stupid to jeopardize our friendship."

"I think we both know that whatever's going on between us goes beyond friendship."

"You noticed, too," he said, the words tinged with sarcasm.

"No more than I'd notice a freight train rushing through my apartment."

Tension charged the atmosphere in the compact car.

"We'd be crazy to get in over our heads," Holly said at last, unable to bear the heavy silence. "You're the first man I've kissed since Craig died. I'm still working on letting him go. And you—"

"I'm the last man in the world any woman should get involved with."

The intensity with which he spoke revealed the depths of his frustration. Holly was glad the street lamp was far enough away that she could see only a faint glimmer in his eyes, and not the true measure of sadness that haunted him. Otherwise, she might do something very foolish.

Very foolish and very wonderful, a little internal voice tormented her.

"Maybe not the *last* man," she said. "There was a pervert who used to lurk around the children's section. I'd take you over him any day."

She'd hoped the note of levity would ease the tension, but he remained serious as he challenged, "How do you know *I'm* not a pervert? For all we know, I could be a serial killer."

"Or married," Holly said, voicing her greatest fear. Although logic told her that serial killers were often quite charming and seemingly innocuous, her heart told her that the man on the seat next to her would never intentionally hurt anyone. But if he was married...

"I'm not married," he said.

"If everything you've told me is true, then you couldn't possibly say that with such certainty."

"You're right," he said. "I can't be certain of anything. And maybe I don't have any right to ask a woman to take my intuition on faith. But—" A harsh groan tore from his throat. He leaned closer and cradled her face in his palm as his eyes locked with hers. "I've given this particular matter a lot of thought, Holly, especially, since I met you. And the only conclusion I've come to is that I couldn't possibly be married to another woman and be drawn to you as strongly as I am."

"But you don't know why you're drawn to me. It could be because I resemble someone you care about."

"I know *exactly* why I'm drawn to you," he said. "And it has *nothing* to do with any other woman."

Holly spread her hand atop his. "It would be so easy to believe that."

Her chest ached with the desire to believe it.

"I may not know my name, or where I came from, but I'm ... *me*," he said. "I think a certain way. I have to believe that I have a certain set of ethical standards that govern my life, regardless of what I call myself or where I live. I lost my memory, but not my morals. Do you remember when I told you about being in the hospital, thinking of that soap-opera character named Craig getting lucky and hoping I could, too?"

Holly nodded.

"I wouldn't think that way if I were married," he said. "Marriage means one man, one woman and a lifetime commitment. I don't have to think about it. That's my attitude toward it. If I were married, it would be for keeps. I wouldn't play around, and I wouldn't be thinking about getting lucky. I might not remember my wife's name any more than I remember my own, but I would damn well remember that I was married."

He read the skepticism in her eyes. "I don't blame you for thinking I'm nuts. Sometimes I wonder if I've lost my mind as well as my memory."

"It's not your sanity I was questioning," she said, lowering her head to hide her face on his shoulder. "It's mine."

She sensed his surprise even in the darkness. "When I met Craig—the man I was engaged to—I was afraid to get involved with him. He was a cop, and I knew what could happen."

A shudder vibrated through her. "But I fell in love with him, anyway, and—" She broke off and drew in a breath before continuing. "My heart shattered into a thousand pieces when he died. Now it seems to be patched together with bailing wire. I don't know if I could put it back together if it got broken again. And yet—"

She lifted her head and peered into his eyes. She didn't move as his face slowly descended to hers, as his mouth claimed hers in a kiss that was brief but intense. And then, as he moved away from her with a regret that almost palpable, a bolt of lightning streaked white-hot through the black sky.

Almost as one, Holly and Craig shivered at the violence of the unexpected flash. Holly wondered if it was static electricity alone that made her scalp prickle or if it was partly pure, unadulterated fear. She was desperately close to falling in love with him, and she had as much as told him so.

Their shock faded into nervous laughter.

"Remind me never to think impure thoughts about you again," Craig quipped.

"I think that was our cue to call it a night," Holly said.

THE FIRST RAINDROPS hit the windshield as Holly turned into the parking lot at her apartment complex a few minutes later. She made a mad dash to her door, slamming it closed behind her as a flash of lightning showed through the windows and a rumble of thunder shook the walls.

She would have loved a long, leisurely bath, but the storm precluded it. Anyone raised in Florida, the lightning capital of the country, knew to stay away from plumbing during thunderstorms. So she thumbed her nose at fate just enough to brush her teeth and wash her face, then put on a satin nightgown, climbed into bed and watched nature's light show outside her window while the rain pelted the roof.

She pulled the covers up under her chin and listened to the wind, the thunder and the rain. Even as a child, Holly had loved storms; she loved the feeling of being inside, safe and dry, while a storm raged just beyond the walls. Tonight, despite the crisp coolness and fresh, clean scent of the bedding, she did not feel so safe. Instead, the turbulence of the weather seemed like a manifestation of her state of mind, an echo of the confusion and fear, the indecision, the sorrow she still felt over Craig's death.

Body aching with the desire for a man's touch, she reached out and took her beloved childhood teddy bear, which ornamented the unused pillow on her bed, and hugged it tight against her. But gone were the days when Teddy could make all the night demons disappear. Closing her eyes against the strobelike light play against her windows, she saw Craig Ford's face as they laughed together watching the movie. She saw the trouble roiling in the depths of his eyes. She tried to remember, but could not, the details of another Craig's face, the rugged male face she had loved so dearly—the face she had expected to find on the pillow next to hers for a full and natural lifetime.

How long she tossed and turned before falling into a troubled sleep, she couldn't have measured. It might have been minutes or it might have been hours. So she didn't know how long she'd slept before the chimes of the doorbell roused her, but she noted in her stuporous state that the faint light of dawn glowed through the windows as she left her bedroom to answer the door. Rain still peppered the roof, but the storm had spent its violence and mellowed into a steady shower.

By the time she'd padded into the living room, she was awake enough to register alarm over the unexpected summons to the door at such an hour, especially in such inclement weather. Just then, the doorbell chimed again, startling her. She made a conscious effort to walk softly so that she did not tip off the person outside that she was approaching the door. She decided use the peephole and dial 911 if she didn't recognize the visitor.

Holding her breath, she stood on tiptoe and peered through the hole, half expecting to see someone big and fierce. But the face she saw was familiar.

The man on her doorstep wasn't wearing a hat; his hair, drenched and dripping, clung to his head. His clothes were saturated and plastered to his body. His skin was also wet; it glistened in the pale morning light. He looked exhausted, troubled and vulnerable. And desperate.

Observing him without his knowledge, Holly shared his desperation, and flung open the door.

"Craig!" she said. "How did you—"

He tilted his head toward a dilapidated bicycle wedged against the railing behind him. "I had to see you. I had to . . ."

His voice trailed off as she reached for his hand and guided him inside. She was in his arms the instant the door closed, offering her mouth to him as she threw her arms around his neck. The embrace was like a spark to dry leaves, the kiss like flame to gasoline.

He was breathless as he dragged his mouth from hers to rasp, "I thought about it all night, Holly. You have too much past, and I don't have any at all. It balances out in some crazy way."

6

STILL EMBRACING, with Holly leading the way, they stumbled to the bathroom. Holly peeled off Craig's shirt and tossed it into the bathtub. Then she plucked a towel from the towel bar and blotted his bare skin, pausing when she discovered an angry, ragged scar running from his left shoulder to his ribs. She lifted her gaze to his questioningly and he shook his head sadly. "It's anybody's guess. It's not from the accident."

Holly draped the towel over his head and dried his hair, massaging briskly.

"Oh, lady," Craig said, the words issuing forth in a sensual rush.

Holly followed his gaze to her chest. Her satin gown, wet from his clothes and translucent as tissue paper, clung to her breasts like a second skin. Her nipples were swollen and firm and perfectly delineated by the pale pink fabric. She gasped as he lifted his hand to cup her left breast, chafing the sensitive tip with his palm.

"If I don't taste you—" He broke off, leaving the consequences of such a dire fate undetailed as he bent to take her right breast into his mouth. He drew on it through the frail satin, flicking his tongue across the beaded nipple.

Holly leaned against the doorjamb for support and wondered how she could have forgotten how sweet it was to have a man kiss her breasts when she remembered her intimate moments with Craig so well. With a languid moan, she closed her eyes and rested her hands on his shoulders while his mouth stoked the flames of desire spreading through her.

He pressed closer, backing her against the wall until his hardness tormented her with the knowledge that he was as aroused as she.

Her thumb grazed the top edge of his scar and she tilted her head to trail the rough ridge of scar tissue with tiny kisses. She heard his sudden inhalation of breath as he slid his hands between the wall and her buttocks and pulled her hard against him.

"There's no other woman," he said. "There can't be. I couldn't feel this way about you if there were." He sealed the declaration with a probing kiss.

Holly felt soft, swollen, boneless, on fire. She clung to him for support, wanting—needing—more from him. She wedged her hand between them to find the waistband of his pants.

Ending the kiss abruptly, Craig covered her hands. "Point of no return, Holly. If you have any intention of stopping—"

She stared into his eyes for what seemed an eternity before grabbing the waistband and yanking open the snap above the zipper. It gave way with a pop that echoed through the small room like "Yes!" shouted across a mountaintop.

She guided the zipper down with a deliberate lack of speed, taking pleasure in the guttural growl that emerged from his throat as she applied subtle pressure to the hot, rock-hard flesh straining against the confinement of his briefs.

After opening the zipper, she hooked her thumbs inside the waistband of his pants, underwear and all, and peeled the soaked fabric down his legs to his ankles. Kneeling, she untied his shoes and he stepped out of them, one by one, and then out of his pants. She drew back her hand to toss them into the bathtub with his shirt, but he looped his hand around her wrist to stop her.

Grabbing the trousers by the band, he searched the back pocket for a small plastic bag folded into a flat rectangle. "I did some shopping on the way over. Just in case."

Holly blushed and diverted her gaze. Although she had a box tucked away in in the drawer of her bedside table and would have insisted that he use a condom, she found it impossible to face that little plastic bag—until he took the pants from her and hurled them into the bathtub, then cupped her chin with his fingertips and guided her face up. Their gazes met and locked. "Just in case," he whispered. "God, Holly, if you knew how much I want you—"

"What makes you think I don't?" she asked, surprising him by coiling her fingers around him and squeezing gently.

He was kissing her before she could register that he had moved. Tasting and plundering. Searching and exploring. Conquering and claiming.

"I can't stand up anymore," she wheezed, pulling her mouth from his with effort.

"I'm not so steady myself," he murmured, nuzzling her neck with moist lips.

Holly inhaled sharply and wrapped her arms around his waist as he caught her earlobe between his teeth and his breath fluttered into her ear. "Holly?"

"Hmm?" she breathed. Her eyes were wide open but she saw him only through a haze of passion.

"Honey, where's the bed?"

"Bed?" she murmured blankly.

He draped his arm across her shoulders. "We'll find it."

The bedroom door was open, the bedside lamp on, gently illumining the rumpled bedding. An artist could not have set up the scene better. The work could have been titled *Invitation to Lovers.*

They stopped next to the bed where the covers were peeled back. Craig tossed the condoms onto the far side of the bed and cradled Holly's head in his hands, combing his fingers through her hair. "Do you know how long I've waited to do this? And then you came to the door with your hair all mussed. You've got to be the sexiest woman alive."

Holly smiled. "You make me feel that way when you look at me."

"You do some pretty remarkable things to me when I look at you."

Holly let her gaze drift downward. "I noticed."

"Wicked woman," he said, dipping his head to kiss her again.

Everything after that was slightly blurred and thoroughly wonderful. Holly could not have asked for a more attentive lover. Tenderly, he lowered her to the bed and eased her gown over her head and arms. He caressed her, sliding his fingers over her skin as if reading her soul in some braillelike code by the way her flesh curved beneath his fingertips. Holly read his body the same way, exploring the curves and textures of his chest and arms, his shoulders and back.

Wonder turned to need, pleasure to urgency, warmth to a consuming inferno as their caresses grew bolder and more intimate. Holly trembled as he sprinkled kisses over her ribs; she quivered with delight as his palm glided up one thigh and down another. He kissed her again, long and hard, then, without warning, he breached the barrier of her panties to probe her depths. She responded with a mindless guttural moan that was both invitation and plea. She strained against his touch with sensual undulations that drew a feral growl of arousal from him.

It seemed an eternity before he removed her panties and eased his hard, sheathed flesh into hers, tempering raw sexual need with patience and consideration.

Embracing, clinging, they moved together, sharing pleasure and sweetness, excitement and splendor.

Holly cried out as the wave of completion swept through her, setting off spasms of release that drove him off the same high cliff. Together they tumbled into the afterglow of sensual bliss.

Minutes later, they lay together, legs entwined, Holly's breasts comfortably crushed against Craig's ribs, his chin tucked to her temple, his arm draped possessively across her waist.

After an absurdly long, divinely serene silence, he said, "Am I your first virgin?"

Recalling the expertise of his technique, she drew an imaginary circle on his chest with her forefinger and said, "You, sir, are no virgin."

"You're the only woman I remember being with."

"Trust me. You're no beginner." She grinned mischievously. "I think we can safely assume that you're heterosexual."

"Trust *me*," he replied. "*That* was never in question." He placed nibbling kisses on her cheek. "I just hope I'm not a priest."

The idea surprised her. "A priest?"

He snuggled down, tightening his arm around her waist and resting his cheek on hers. "I could never go back to celibacy after being with you."

"Think what a test of faith that would be," she said.

"I'll just have to become a Protestant," he said, hooking his leg over hers.

Holly closed her eyes and enjoyed the sheer joy of being with a man in such an intimate way. He seemed to surround her completely, and she felt safe for the first time since she'd gotten the phone call from Josh telling her to get to the hospital as quickly as possible.

She knew the safety was an illusion—how much safety could there be with a man with no name and no past?—but she allowed herself to believe because believing felt so good. "How can you joke about it?" she asked.

"The amnesia?"

She nodded. "It must be horrible for you not knowing anything about yourself."

"I can't do a damn thing about it," he said. "Sometimes I get a headache from trying so hard to concentrate. I keep thinking that if I could concentrate hard enough, I'll remember something. But there's nothing but odd bits of information that pop up from time to time to give me a hint."

"Like knowing about wine."

"Like knowing about wine." He exhaled heavily and reflexively tightened his arm around her. His voice was flat with intensity. "If I didn't joke about it, I'd go crazy."

"I wish I could help."

He pushed a strand of hair from her cheek and tucked it behind her ear. "You *are* helping." She saw the haunting darkness in his gaze as he looked deeply into her eyes. "You're my touchstone with reality. Everything else is just assumption or supposition."

So he needed her as much as she needed him. It was not such a bad foundation for an affair, she decided. Maybe he'd been right about things balancing out between them in some cockeyed way. She lifted her hand to his face and touched it lovingly with her fingertips. "How would you like to make another memory?"

His mouth curved into a smile. Desire glinted in his eyes. "I'd like to fill my entire empty memory bank with images of you."

"One memory at a time," she said, guiding his mouth to hers.

They made love again, taking the time that urgency had denied them earlier, familiarizing themselves with each other, building toward physical release by placing kisses upon touches, sighs upon whispered entreaties and, ultimately, frenzied thrust upon frenzied thrust.

Spent, exhausted and utterly content, they collapsed into each other's arms with mingled sighs. Minutes passed before Craig breached the silence by voicing her name in a question.

"Hmm?" she replied from a dreamlike haze of contentment.

"That's going to be a very precious memory."

"Mmm," she agreed. "For me, too." She could almost feel the process of letting go as the present insinuated itself on the past, not replacing the times she'd spent with the first Craig, but bullying old memories into perspective, labeling them as The Past and forcing them into a corner already occupied with high school dances and flirting with lifeguards on the beach.

"I know it's late," he said.

"I hope you're not suggesting that I should get out of bed and drive you home."

She felt the tension claim his body. "I don't consider that Victorian cracker box home. It's just where I live because I don't have any other place to go. And if I were hell-bent on getting there at this hour, I'd pedal there on my own steam the way I got here."

The bitter overtone in his voice disturbed her. And touched her. "What then?"

"This is going to sound strange."

"Out with it," she said.

"I'm suddenly starving. You don't have any ice cream, do you?"

A quiver marched up her spine to prickle her scalp. "Ice cream?"

"I just suddenly had a yen for it."

Craig had always wanted ice cream after sex. She'd kept a carton in the freezer for him.

"I'm sorry, I . . . don't have any," she said. Throwing out the half-empty carton which had been in her freezer since the last time she and Craig had been together had been a therapeutic step in her determined effort to move on with her life. She'd stood next to the garbage can with the ice-encrusted carton chilling her hands for a full ten minutes before forcing herself to let it drop into the plastic-lined can.

He shrugged. "It was a crazy idea, anyway."

"There's a convenience store on the corner," she suggested helpfully.

He climbed out of bed and walked to the window. Holly admired the lithe lines of his long body and sleek shoulders as he parted the drapes half an inch to peer out. "It's not raining anymore," he said. "If I had some dry clothes, I'd go get some."

Holly imagined his clothing wet and crumpled in the bathtub, then remembered the sealed plastic bags in the storage shed.

Give Craig's clothes to the man who'd taken Craig's place in her bed? Reflexively, she balked at the idea. It would be insanity. Sheer insanity.

But a small, pragmatic voice inside her asked, *Why not?* They were perfectly good clothes and they weren't doing anyone any good where they were. She'd been planning on taking them to a shelter so someone would get some use out of them. Why shouldn't it be Craig Ford? He didn't have a lot of clothes, and he certainly wasn't going to build much of a wardrobe on a shelving assistant's salary.

Her nightgown lay at the foot of the bed. Tucking the sheet under her arms, she crawled down to get it and slipped it over her head. Then she got out of bed, smoothing the gown over her hips as she stood up. "I think I have a solution to the problem."

"Are you sure?" he asked when she presented him with the bags and a brief explanation.

She nodded. "Absolutely. Now go see if anything fits. I'm going to see if there's any juice in the refrigerator."

A little while later, he stood in the doorway to the kitchen in a T-shirt with a charity fun run logo on the chest and a pair of denim shorts. Spreading his arms awkwardly, he said, "Well?"

"Great!"

He gave her a long, hard look. "Are you really okay with this?"

She nodded, surprised that it didn't really bother her. "The shirt was a freebie. Craig never wore it. He hated yellow. And the shorts are looser on you."

Her fiancé had worn denim like a second skin over his well-developed thighs. This Craig was longer and leaner.

"The shoes are a perfect fit. They look brand-new."

The image of Craig's worn sneakers on the shelf in her closet passed through Holly's mind. She steeled herself against the pain of remembering and said, "They are. His mother sent them to him for Christmas and they were too big. He never got around to exchanging them." A bittersweet smile played at her mouth. "He kept saying he'd just wear two pairs of socks with them, but I didn't believe it for a minute. The only time he wore socks off duty was at the gym, and he kept a special pair of shoes in his locker there." She paused for a moment, then said, "Would you like a glass of orange juice?"

He shook his head. "No, thanks. It might ruin my palate for the ice cream."

She was suddenly aware of his eyes on her in a frankly sensual way. She tried to smile as if she were used to parading around in front of men in her nightgown, but she felt the heat rising in her cheeks.

"Hey, don't blush," he said, crossing the narrow room to slide his arms around her waist. When she didn't look at him, he raised his right hand to cup her chin and tilt her face toward his. "You have nothing to be embarrassed about, Holly. You're beautiful. And sexy. I was just thinking what a lucky man I am to have been with you." His voice softened. "And thinking how incredible it is that we haven't been out of bed half an hour and I want you all over again."

With his arm firmly around her waist, and her breasts covered by only a thin stretch of satin pressed against the hard warmth of his chest, she was beginning to feel the same way. "You'd better go get that ice cream," she said.

"Send me off with a kiss."

She laughed. "You're going to the corner for ice cream, not into battle."

"It's a cold, cruel world out there," he said, sprinkling tender, teasing kisses over her eyelids.

Capturing his face in her palms, she stood on tiptoe to kiss him briefly, then said with the sultry tone of an old screen siren, "Hurry back, big boy."

When he left, Holly considered dressing for the day, then reconsidered and decided to remain in her gown. It was still early morning, and her troubled sleep, capped by Craig Ford's unexpected visit and subsequent events had left her enervated. Pulling an afghan up to her shoulders, she cuddled into the corner of the sofa to await Craig's return, feeling thoroughly lazy and self-indulgent.

When she answered his knock a few minutes later, she found him leaning nonchalantly against the doorjamb with a cocky grin on his face. He carried a pint of gourmet rocky road in one hand and two plastic spoons in the other.

He followed her to the couch, where she curled into the corner again. He sat down next to her and guided her legs across the tops of his thighs. "You can put one of those spoons down," Holly said. "I refuse to eat rocky road ice cream for breakfast."

But her resolve lasted only until he'd made a production of swallowing several spoonfuls with exaggerated gestures and sounds of ecstasy, then teasingly passing a loaded spoon under her nose, dotting her lips with ice cream and leaning over to flick the stain away with his tongue. After that, they shared the ice cream, jousting for space in the carton with their spoons, feeding each other, kissing the remnants of the rich confection from each other's lips.

By the time the ice-cream carton was empty, they were beyond caring. They barely made it back to the bedroom before making love again. Afterward, they collapsed into a tangle of arms and legs and slept until well past noon.

They were still there when the doorbell rang. "Expecting company?" Craig asked.

"No," she said, scrambling out of bed and digging frantically through a drawer in search of clothing. "It's probably one of my neighbors."

She threw on a pair of shorts and a shirt and went to the door, finger-combing her hair along the way. She heard Craig stumble into the living room behind her as she looked through the peephole. Turning, she saw that he'd gotten dressed and was hopping, trying to tie his shoelace as he walked. "It's Josh, Craig's partner. The one who's checking the missing persons reports. He might have news."

She disengaged the chain lock, but hesitated before opening the door. "This could be a bit awkward," she warned Craig.

It wasn't going to take much for Josh to figure out that she and Craig Ford had slept together. They both looked rumpled and smug. Josh, with his eye for incriminating detail, would pick up on it immediately.

Then Josh's voice, with a note of concern. "Holly?"

Holly opened the door. "Hi, Josh."

"What gives?" he asked, bustling past her. "I was beginning to think someone was holding you hostage."

Holly tried to sound nonchalant despite the boorish, you'd-better-explain yourself look Josh gave her. "Josh, this is Craig Ford, from the library. He's the person I told you about. Craig—"

She was spared further responsibility for the introduction when Josh extended his hand to Craig and identified himself. Holly sensed testosterone-fed animosity crackling in the air as the two men pumped hands and stared at each other with thinly veiled suspicion.

"Can I get you something to drink, Josh?" she offered brightly, hoping to distract him.

"Not unless you have a beer handy."

"As a matter of fact, I do," Holly said. She'd bought a six-pack after Josh's last visit, in case he dropped in again. "I'll get one for you."

But Josh didn't appear to hear her. His eyes were riveted on Craig's chest. "Where did you get that shirt?"

Craig looked down at the shirt he'd just put on, but before he could answer, Josh challenged, "The only way to get a shirt like that was to run in that event. Since you have the shirt, maybe—"

His gaze shifted to Holly. "Unless *you* gave it to him."

Taken aback by his accusatory tone, Holly was slow forming a reply. Before she could offer an explanation, he said, "You did!"

"Holly was just being helpful," Craig said.

"His clothes were wet," Holly said.

"So you gave him Craig's shirt?"

"It's not a crime, Josh," she said, glaring at him. "You can lose the tough-cop attitude. You're among friends. Why don't you sit down while I get that beer."

"I'll help you get it," Josh said, giving Craig a quelling look when he moved to accompany them.

Craig's gaze flew to Holly's face. She shrugged and mouthed, "It's okay." Reluctantly, he walked to the couch and sat down. Holly steeled herself for a confrontation and proceeded into the kitchen.

Josh didn't bother with tact. "Just what do you think you're doing?" he demanded.

"Getting you a beer," she said with forced calm.

"You know what I mean. What's going on between you and Pretty Boy out there?"

She thrust a can in his hand. "I'm not going to pretend I don't know what you're talking about. I'll tell you what's going on. Exactly what it looks like, that's what's going on."

"Are you *nuts?* The guy is as phony as a three-dollar bill."

Her eyes narrowed. "Did you find out something?"

"No! That's why I'm convinced he's not for real. There's nothing."

"I believe his story," she said.

"If you believed it, you wouldn't have been so ready to believe that I'd found out something just now."

"I was *hoping* you'd found out something," Holly said. "I *care* about him."

"Enough to sleep with him?"

"My bedroom is none of your business."

"You're the one who brought me into this."

"I asked for your help, not—"

"You aren't listening to me."

"You don't know him the way I do."

His laugh was almost a sneer. "Not quite."

"You could trust my judgment, you know."

"Your *judgment?* You're dressing him in Craig's clothes and playing house with him! You're thinking below the waist, Holly."

Holly stiffened her spine and glared at him. "If I didn't think you were sincerely concerned about me, I'd slap your face for that."

After a second or two of stunned silence, he shook his head, shrugged, popped the tab on the top of the beer can and took a generous swig. "I don't trust any man who doesn't drink beer."

"He's more the wine type."

"I rest my case."

"Oh, grow up!" Holly said, rolling her eyes and stalking past him into the living room.

Craig snapped to attention as Holly approached. She smiled reassuringly, as though she'd known how difficult it had been for him to let her go off alone with Josh, even if just into the next room.

He forced himself to return her smile, wishing he could talk to her alone. He'd distinguished only isolated words coming from the next room, but he had a good idea what had been discussed, and he didn't like her having to explain herself or defend her relationship with him to anybody.

She sat on the sofa close to where he'd been sitting, and scooted even closer once he was settled next to her. Then she picked up his hand and sandwiched it between hers on her thigh. Craig couldn't escape the feeling that her actions were a display of loyalty in front of her fiancé's partner, which only confirmed that he'd been right about her need to defend her relationship with him.

"Scalisi promised to let me know if there were any developments," Craig said, a little defensively.

"A good-looking guy like you drops out of sight, and nobody seems to notice," Josh said, folding his long frame into an armchair. "It's odd, isn't it?"

"It's hell on a man's ego," Craig replied evenly, trying not to respond too belligerently to the challenging tone Josh had used. He didn't want to provoke him. The guy was trouble; Craig could feel it in his guts. Holly had meant well when she'd asked for the man's help, but he wished she hadn't. He didn't need a cop with an attitude complicating things, particularly one with a proprietary interest in Holly.

"Scalisi and I are double-checking the MP reports that come in," Josh said. "MP—that's *missing persons*."

"I'm familiar with the jargon by now," Craig said.

"I'll just bet you are," Josh said, dripping sarcasm.

"Josh!" Holly said.

Craig squeezed her hand. "You don't have to defend me, Holly. I can speak for myself." He leveled his gaze on Josh. "You seem to have a problem with my situation."

"A problem? I don't have a problem with it. I just don't buy it."

"J—" Holly swallowed the second half of the syllable when Craig gave her hand another squeeze.

"I appreciate your candor," Craig said. "Do you mind telling me why you feel the way you do?"

"It just doesn't play," Josh said. "No one drops out of sight without being missed unless he plans it that way."

Craig pondered the comment before answering. "You've been a cop too long, buddy. If I wanted to disappear, I'd disappear to a tropical island or a mountaintop somewhere. I'm living in limbo here."

The lewd glint in the cop's eyes as his gaze slid to Holly made Craig want to cram a fist down Josh's throat, especially when he said, "From my perspective, it doesn't look like you're doing all that bad."

"My relationship with Holly has nothing to do with my amnesia. I've lost my memory, but not my ability to feel, and my feelings for Holly are genuine."

"How touching."

"Josh!" Holly repeated, pulling her hand free. "I came to you in friendship asking for help. If you want to help, then help. If not, tell me to go jump off a cliff. But don't come into my home and insult someone I care about."

Frowning, Josh regarded them for several seconds. With the forced sincerity of a political hostage compelled to betray his cause, he said, "I may have come on a bit strong. If I did, I'm sorry."

"Apology accepted," Holly said, visibly relaxing.

Josh addressed Craig. "You know about Craig?"

He nodded.

"He was my best friend as well as my partner," Josh explained. "That makes Holly... Let's just say, I wouldn't want to see her hurt."

"Then we have that much in common," Craig said, spreading his arm across Holly's shoulders. "Hurting Holly is the last thing I'd ever want to do."

"Assuming that your story is solid and you do have amnesia, have you given any thought to what's going to happen if you wake up one morning and remember that you have a pregnant wife and a couple of kids?"

"Craig doesn't think he's married," Holly said.

As the words left her mouth, she realized how naive they sounded.

"Well, for your sake, I hope to hell he's right about that," Josh said. "Either, way, I'm going to be monitoring the missing persons reports very closely."

7

DAYLIGHT WAS FADING, the sun disappearing on the western horizon. The crowd on the beach had thinned, and the rhythmic lap of the ocean and the caw of soaring gulls were gradually replacing the sounds of human frolicking.

Craig and Holly lay side by side on beach chairs, resting from an hour of serious play in the waves. Holly's hair was beginning to dry, and the breeze sweeping gently over the surf lifted tendrils around her face. The fingers of her right hand were threaded through the fingers of Craig's left. Her eyes were closed.

"This was a good idea," she said.

"Excellent," Craig agreed, sounding as mellow as she felt.

"I had to get out of the apartment after that scene with Josh."

"He means well," Craig said.

Holly laughed softly. "I was just about to say the same thing. If I had known he was going to be such a jerk, I wouldn't have called him."

"He's just trying to protect you."

"He feels responsible for me."

Seconds ticked by in silence before he said, "What if he's right? What if I'm wrong about being married? What if I'm a bigger jerk than he is, and I'm believing what I want to believe because I'm head over heels in lust with you?"

What if? Holly had asked herself the same questions over and over. And every time she asked the question, she gave herself the same answer she now gave him: "If it works out that way, then we'll deal with it."

"What if I'm such a creep that I can't deal with the memories of what I'm really like, so I'm making up an idealized personality for myself?" His tone was tortured. "What if everyone who knows me either doesn't care what happened to me or is so glad I'm gone that they just haven't bothered to report it?"

Tightening her fingers around his, Holly said, "You are who you are and what you are."

He twisted his head toward hers and studied her face. "We don't know who I am."

She was never immune to that haunting loneliness in his eyes. "We know *what* you are," she said. "That's more important than names."

"Tell me, Holly," he said grimly. "What am I?"

"Kind. Witty. Gentle." She smiled. "Passionate."

"How do we know that the man you know is the real me? Maybe the man you know is some reverse image of who I really am."

"How would I know that about any man?" Holly asked. "The papers are filled with stories about men who deceive women, who live double lives, who have Jekyll-and-Hyde personalities. At least with you, I know where the question marks are."

Seconds passed before he said, "I can't remember anything before a few weeks ago, but I can't believe that I could ever have felt as much affection for a woman as I feel for you at this moment."

Holly's smile was bittersweet. "I'm your touch-stone, remember?"

He looked into her eyes. "That I could never forget."

TUESDAY AFTERNOON, Meryl and Sarah cornered Holly in the ladies' room, demanding details.

"Details of what?" Holly asked, feigning innocence.

"Details of what, she wants to know!" Meryl said.

"Start with the skink and then explain why neither of us heard from you all weekend," Sarah said.

"And why you've had that smug, cat-with-a-canary expression on your face," Meryl said.

"I plead my Fifth Amendment right not to answer," Holly said.

"I knew it!" Sarah said.

"That explains why you and Craig have been play-ing peek-and-grin all day," Meryl said. "He can't take his eyes off you!"

"He never could," Sarah teased. "But now Holly can't take her eyes off him, either. I wonder why."

"Do you think all three of us should be in here at the same time?" Holly said. "Who's running the library?"

"You're right," Sarah said with an aggrieved sigh. "Meryl and I are absent without leave, so you're off the hook for now."

"But only until lunch tomorrow."

"Lunch tomorrow?" Holly said.

"The poor dear's so addled she doesn't remember that we have lunch every Wednesday," Meryl said.

"Tomorrow's Wednesday?" Holly asked.

"She's got it bad," Sarah said, shaking her head.

"Ba-a-a-d," Meryl agreed. "But we'll just have to wait until tomorrow to find out all about it."

"And you know the rule," Sarah said. "No Fifth Amendment protection at Wednesday lunch."

"That's never been a rule," Holly protested.

"It's new," Sarah said.

"Since when?"

"Since Sarah made it up," Meryl said. "Come on, Sarah. We'll just have to keep our curiosity on hold until tomorrow."

"And it had better be good!" Sarah said.

"With juicy details," Meryl added.

A few minutes later, at her desk, Holly spied Craig in the general fiction section. She bit her tongue to keep from laughing aloud as he pulled a silly face.

As Meryl had noted, they'd been playing peek-and-grin all day. Sometimes he winked. Sometimes he made a face. And, when he was sure no one else was looking, he stuck out his tongue or threw her a kiss.

Holly felt alive for the first time since her fiancé's death. She felt about thirteen years old. She felt giddy. She felt . . . *wonderful*.

At lunch the next day, she confessed to her friends that she and Craig had become lovers. Meryl and Sarah did everything but produce pom-poms and lead the entire restaurant in a rousing cheer.

"So, out with it—how was it?" Meryl prodded.

"It was . . . *nice*." The understatement took on strength as it came out sounding suspiciously like a sigh of contentment.

"Oh, come on!" Sarah said. "We're living vicariously here."

"Sorry," Holly said. "That's all I have to say."

"Awwww!" Sarah groaned, leaning forward to bash her forehead against the table several times. "She's not going to tell us anything."

"At least give us a scale reading," Meryl said. "One to ten."

"Ten being maximum?" Holly asked.

Meryl nodded, and Sarah, apparently unharmed by the head bashing, squealed delightedly, "She wants to know the maximum!"

Holly paused for dramatic impact, then, with a dumb grin on her face, said, "Twenty-five."

"I knew it!" Sarah said.

Meryl propped her chin on her fist and issued a lengthy sigh. "So did I."

"He's going to help me out at Story Hour tomorrow," Holly said, deftly changing the subject. "We're doing fairy-tale classics. He agreed to read the part of the Big Bad Wolf."

A beat of silence passed before Meryl and Sarah both chuckled, and Meryl asked, "Does he know about the ears and the—" She flapped her hand back and forth, suggesting the swish of a tail.

"I might have forgotten to mention the . . . uh, costume," Holly admitted.

"You're evil," Meryl said, gleefully wringing her hands together. "I can hardly wait to see it."

"See it?" Sarah asked. "I'm going to tape it for our video library!"

CRAIG GRUMBLED a bit about the fuzzy fake-fur ears and the bushy tail suspended from an elastic belt, but he took some consolation in the fact that Holly would be wearing a pink plastic snout as well as ears and a ridiculous curly tail for her portrayal of the Three Little Pigs.

He charmed the children from the first "I swear by the hair on my chinny-chin-chin" down to the final "I'll huff, and I'll puff, and I'll *bl-o-o-o-w* your house in!" In fact, Holly was certain he'd added an extra "o" and got a little more flamboyant with each repetition. He even managed to make his death wails comical, upon sliding down the chimney into the pot of boiling water the pigs had waiting for him.

As an encore, Holly traded her snout and ears for a red plastic cape for a reading of "Little Red Riding Hood." Everything went smoothly until she got to Grandma's house, and then it seemed to her that the Big Bad Wolf might possibly be having a bit *too much* fun in his role. The children, involved in the story, didn't seem to notice the sensual gleam in his eyes as she exclaimed, "Oh, Grandma, what big eyes you have!" Nor did they seem to hear the suggestion in his voice as he answered, "The better to see you with, my dear."

Holly's voice caught in her throat as she read, "Oh, Grandma! What big teeth you have!"

The gleam glinted even brighter, the suggestion grew thicker as he replied, "The better to eat you with, *my dear.*" He turned the remark into an erotic promise that sent fire spreading through Holly, turning the storybook endearment into an intimate caress that made her cheeks flame and her knees weak.

She welcomed the rowdy applause that followed the conclusion of the story, glad that the children's enchantment with his portrayal of the wolf had apparently distracted them from noticing her odd behavior. "I'm going to get you for this," she said under her breath as she extended her arm, gesturing for him to take a bow.

He grinned diabolically. "Tomorrow night?"

They were planning on going to an early movie straight from the library, and Holly had little doubt they'd end up at her apartment afterward. Giving him a dose of his own medicine, she smiled seductively. "Maybe. If I'm in the mood."

"You'll be in the mood," he said, bowing to his adoring audience again. Then, pleading that he had to go back to work, he waved goodbye to the kids and walked away with ears pointed high and tail swishing.

When the crowd had dispersed, Holly walked to the corner where Sarah was packing away the camera equipment. "Craig was great, wasn't he? Did you get it all on tape?"

"It'll be the first X-rated story hour in our collection," Sarah replied drolly.

"Was it that obvious?" Holly asked, mortified.

Sarah chuckled. "Only if you were looking for it."

The rest of the workday passed quickly, and before Holly realized that it was almost closing time, Craig showed up to help her put the children's section in order. "Are you in the mood yet?" he asked as they sorted.

"Not yet," she said, continuing her work as though she gave the matter no importance at all.

Liar! Craig thought. She was as much in the mood as he was. He could tell from her voice, and the way she'd avoided looking at him when she said it. Holly almost always looked a person square in the eyes when she spoke to him. "I was thinking that if you were, we might...open a bottle of wine or something after work."

"Maybe after the movie tomorrow night," she said.

Craig bit back a smile. There was no conviction in her voice. She was playing hard-to-get, talk-me-into-it. But talking wasn't exactly what he had in mind.

"You're probably right," he said, feigning the same lack of interest she was displaying. "We have to be at work early tomorrow morning."

Later, he walked her to her car and kissed her goodnight. Quite thoroughly. Giving her something to think about. He felt her melting in his arms, softening, responding. Oh, yeah. She was going to be thinking about him, all right.

Holly let the engine warm up longer than usual after getting in the car, but whether she was letting the engine warm up or giving herself a chance to cool down, she wasn't quite sure. What a kiss!

What a man! It was enough to make her want to leap out of the car, kidnap him and take him home with her. Actually, she'd been a little disappointed when he'd given up so easily on the idea of getting together tonight. True, they'd been together most of the weekend as well as Monday and Tuesday night—together in the most significant and sweetest sense of the word. That had left her with Wednesday morning free for her to sleep late and wash her hair before meeting Meryl and Sarah for lunch.

And Wednesday night for her to start missing Craig.

Scowling, she put the car into gear and headed out of the parking lot. He could have argued just a little.

At home, she fed the cat, took a shower, threw on her frivolous boxer shorts-and-baseball-shirt pinstriped pajamas and curled up on the sofa. Buttercup joined her, poking her nose at Holly's hand until Holly petted her. Gradually, the cat rolled onto her back and Holly stroked her chest. After a minute or two, the cat unexpectedly rolled back over, strolled to the other end of the couch, threw a perplexed look at Holly over her shoulder and meowed angrily.

"What's wrong, Buttercup? You miss him, too?" Holly exhaled a sigh. "How quickly we get used to—"

Her banter was cut short by a series of forceful knocks at the door. Alarmed, she looked at the wall clock. Ten after ten. Too late for casual visitors. As if any casual visitor would be making such a racket. After a moment of uncertainty, she crept to the door and apprehensively stood on tiptoe to look out the peephole.

Just as she was about to position her eye, the knocking started again. Startled, she gasped, then clasped her hands over her mouth, not wanting to make any sound that would betray her presence to the unknown person on the other side of the door. Holding her breath, she tried again, then gasped once more in surprise. The gasp quickly grew into bubbling laughter when she saw who was beating on her door so rudely.

It was the Big Bad Wolf.

At least, her visitor had ears like the Big Bad Wolf. And she suspected that if she could see the proper location for such a thing, he'd have a bushy tail, as well.

Playing games, was he? She opened the door as far as the chain latch permitted and stuck her face into the crack. "Oh, my!"

"Open the door and let me in."

"My mother told me never to open my door to wolves," Holly replied.

"Open the door and let me in, or I swear by the hair on my chinny-chin-chin that I'll huff, and I'll puff, and I'll blow your house in!"

"Or wake up all my neighbors," Holly said, undoing the chain. She'd been right about the tail. It swished proudly behind him as he walked.

"I can't believe you—*Craig?*"

He was staring at her. Lewdly. "The name is Wolf," he said, closing the space between them so he could pull her into his arms roughly. *"Big—"* He nibbled on her neck above her pajama top. *"Bad—"* His hands slid under her top to knead her bare back. *"Wolf."*

He pressed her against the door and kissed her as though he'd been waiting a century for the taste of her. His mouth and hands were greedy and restless, persistent and relentless. "Sweet little girls like you shouldn't let wolves in," he wheezed, as he kissed his way to the top button of her shirt. "You could get eaten up."

"What big hands you have, Mr. Wolf," she said. *What naughty hands!* What *wonderful* hands.

"The better to take off your clothes with," he said, pulling his hands from inside the back of her shirt to undo the buttons. The fronts parted, and he shoved her pajama top down over her shoulders, baring her from the waist up. He stared at her breasts with the same hunger with which he'd kissed her.

"What . . . big *eyes* you have," she murmured, feeling his gaze as vividly as she would a touch, tasting his desire on her tongue, which still tingled from the touch of his.

"The better to see you with," he said, pushing her boxer shorts down until the elastic cleared her hips and floated to the floor, leaving her clad only in her bikini panties.

He tossed his head back and howled, then slapped his hands over her buttocks and pulled her against him.

Holly slid her arms around his waist and cupped his behind as he was cupping hers. She looked up at him and licked her lips very slowly. "Oh, Mr. Wolf—what a big...*bushy tail*," she said as the synthetic fur brushed the tops of her fingers.

"The better to . . . tickle you with."

"But Mr. Wolf—I'm not ticklish."

He bowed his head to kiss the spot where her neck sloped into her shoulder, then moved steadily upward until he reached her ear. "I don't believe you."

"I'm n—" Her protest was swallowed by surprise when he unexpectedly bent at the waist, thrust his shoulder into her midsection, stretched his arm across the backs of her knees and lifted her the way a fireman would.

He took her only as far as the couch, then tossed her on her back and stood over her, unfastening the belt that held the tail. "Not ticklish, huh?" he asked.

Holly shook her head.

"How about here?" he said, flicking the tip of the tail over her instep.

She issued a totally female squeak and pulled her foot away. He whisked the fur over her other foot.

"That's a blatant abuse of county property!" she said.

He looked down at her and grinned diabolically. "I'm the Big Bad Wolf, sweetmeats. I don't give a damn about county property."

To prove it, he dragged the tail up her shin, past her knee, over her thigh, up to her midriff, then circled her breasts. Finally, as she held her breath in anticipation, he teased the hairy tip over her nipples until she wondered if a woman could die from pure arousal.

It was not just the feather softness of the fake tail driving her to the edge of madness. It was the way he caressed her with his eyes, memorizing her, adoring her. It was the way he moved with deliberate slowness, as if he had nothing else in the world to do except pleasure her. It was the way his eyes darkened to a velvety blue and he smiled gently, as if there was nothing else he'd rather be doing. It was being almost naked and feeling vulnerable when he was fully dressed, but trusting, deep in her heart, that he would not hurt her.

"Did you notice my big teeth?" he said.

Words lodged in Holly's throat when she tried to speak, but she managed to nod.

"They're to bite little girls with," he said. He drew the tail along her shoulder. "I'm especially fond of shoulders."

He let her feel his teeth as he nipped her flesh again and again, never punishing, apologizing with a kiss after every nibble. "Ah! Fingers!" he said. "I love fingers." He pretended to gobble them, but licked and sucked instead.

Holly wanted to tell him how magic his touch was, but when she tried to speak, *I* sounded more like, *Ahhhh,* and everything else got lost in a sigh.

"The advantage of big ears," Craig said, pausing to study her face, "is being able to hear the sweet little sounds you make."

Releasing her hand, he grabbed her ankle and guided it to his mouth. Then, growling fiercely, he bit her instep playfully. Still growling, he gnawed on the fullness of her calf before moving higher to abuse her knee with a series of little nips.

"You smell like flowers," he said, his voice wavering enough to show that he was not unaffected by his play.

"Bath . . . gel," Holly said breathlessly.

"Uh-uh," he replied, before sliding his tongue up her thigh. "You." He nibbled then, pinching tender flesh with his teeth just until she was aware of the pressure, tantalizing and torturing with sensation that spread tendrils of fire through her.

He rose, removed his shirt and tossed it aside, then grinned down at her as he reached for the snap on his jeans. "Do you know what else big bad wolves have?"

"Show me," she whispered hoarsely.

Seconds later, he stood in front of her, proud, virile and magnificent.

Spreading her arms in invitation, she said, "I'm yours, Mr. Wolf."

He stared at her a moment, drinking in her beauty, scalding her with the bold yearning in his gaze. "Sweetmeats, this wolf is going to eat you up."

He joined her on the couch, threading his fingers into her hair and kissing her while his weight pinned her to the cushions. As the heat of their bodies merged in an inferno of need and yearning, Holly's last conscious thought was that the fire between them might consume them both.

SHE AWOKE EARLY the next morning and stole out of bed, careful not to disturb Craig, who was still sleeping soundly. Sometime during the night they'd moved from the couch to the bedroom. Standing next to him, she looked at his face for a long moment, moved almost to tears by the male beauty of his features, wondering how many women had looked at him the same way, with the same swelling of affection for him. She imagined him as a small boy, with plumpness in his cheeks instead of the shadow of dark beard. His hair would have looked the same, rumpled and unruly. Had his mother stood next to his bed, looking at him the way she was doing now? She could not imagine that a man with his humor and innate kindness could have been raised without the warmth of humor and kindness in his life.

Where is your mother now? she asked silently. *Why hasn't she reported you missing?*

She tiptoed to the dresser and eased open the drawer, taking out what she would need after her shower, then crept to the bathroom with a sly smile curving her lips,

Half an hour later, Craig was roused by three juvenile voices singing, "Who's Afraid of the Big Bad Wolf?" Groaning, he rolled over to check on the source and saw the tape player on the floor. Next to the tape player was a pair of black high-heeled pumps. Emerging from the shoes were shapely legs encased in shimmery black stockings held up by lace-trimmed garter tabs suspended from a black-and-red strapless garment of see-through lace. The bustier hugged lush female curves.

The woman in the garment was leaning against the wall, twirling a bushy tail in her hand like a stripper with a long strand of pearls. Wolf ears sprouted from hair that looked as if she'd just emerged from bed, and her lips glistened cherry red.

He stared. And stared.

She continued to twirl the tail. "What the matter, *Big Bad?*" she said. "Haven't you ever seen a She-Wolf before?"

8

"HOLLY."

An ominous note in Sarah's voice sent shivers of dread up Holly's spine. She looked up from the stack of new books she was working on. "What is it?"

There was nothing reassuring in Sarah's manner as she replied, "You're wanted in the break room." She hesitated, chewing on her bottom lip, before adding, "It's . . . Craig."

It couldn't have happened again, Holly thought frantically. Not twice to the same woman in a single lifetime. She couldn't even bear to think about it. "But I just saw him. He was in the stacks. He can't be—"

"He's okay. Physically, I mean. But something's going on. Two cops—one of them is Craig's old partner. I can't remember his name."

"Josh," Holly said,

"They came to the front desk and asked if there was somewhere they could talk to Craig privately. Now they're asking for you, too."

Holly felt as though she'd turned to wood. Getting out of the chair required concentrated effort.

"Holly?"

Holly's gaze met her friend's.

"Are you in some kind of trouble?"

Holly shook her head. "I'm not in trouble with the law, if that's what you mean." Emotional trouble was a different matter; one Holly didn't want to discuss.

"It's just," Sarah said, "we don't really know much about Craig."

Not facts, Holly thought. She didn't even know his real name. But, deep in her heart, she knew the man he was, the person he was, as well as she'd ever known anyone.

"Don't jump to wild conclusions," Holly said. "It's probably not at all what it looks like."

Sarah frowned. "Well, if you ever want to talk it over, you know Meryl and I—"

"I know," Holly said. "And I'll explain once I know what's going on."

The door to the break room, usually open, was closed. Holly swallowed the lump in her throat, then knocked tentatively.

Josh opened the door. "Holly. Good. I think you need to hear this, and your . . . *friend* has agreed to have you listen in."

"Craig?" Holly said, catching sight of him. He was seated at the table in the center of the room, his face pale and skin ashen.

"And this is Mick Scalisi," Josh said. "He's in charge of the John Doe case."

Scalisi, a stocky man with graying black hair, held out his hand. "Nice to meet you."

Holly shook his hand, but her attention was focused on Craig, and it was to him she addressed her question. "What's this about?"

Craig drew in a deep breath and released it wearily.

"Show her," Josh ordered.

"Craig?" she asked, apprehension choking her. She'd always been able to read his frame of mind through his eyes, and his eyes were tragic and defeated as he picked up a sheet of paper on the table in front of him and held it out to her. With trembling fingers, she took what appeared to be a computer-generated form.

"It's a missing persons report that came in this morning," Josh said. "Take a look at the description."

She read it with growing unease. Age: 32. Height: 6 feet, 3 inches. Hair: black. Eyes: blue. Distinguishing marks: scar on left chest extending to shoulder.

Her gaze locked with Craig's. "It sounds like you."

"Check out the last date seen," Josh said.

It was over two months earlier. "I'm sorry," she said, shaking her head in rejection of the entire situation. "Is that supposed to be significant?"

"It was a week before my accident," Craig said.

"Then it could be you," Holly said, settling into a chair next to his and reaching for his hands. "This is good news, isn't it?"

His eyes told her it wasn't. For that matter, so did the grim faces of Josh and Scalisi. "What?" she asked, wishing with every fiber of her being that she didn't have to hear.

"He's married," Josh said. "His wife filed the report."

"They aren't sure about anything yet," Craig said, curling his fingers around hers.

"Six foot three," Josh said. "Scar on the chest. Same hair. Same eyes."

"We haven't verified anything," Scalisi said. He turned to Holly. "We faxed a photo to the authorities in Virginia. They're going to have the wife take a look at them."

"I talked to the officer in charge of the case in Virginia," Josh said. "Wifey didn't report him missing right away because she threw him out. They went to a party, had a little too much to drink and she took exception to his flirting with another woman. They fought when they got home and he popped her one, giving her a black eye."

"Craig would never do anything like that," Holly said.

Dismissing her protest with a shrug, Josh continued, "He left on a two-week sales trip the next day, and she told him not to bother coming back. She insists she never really thought he'd stay away. Apparently, this wasn't the first time they'd been through some rough waters. Or the first black eye."

"It's not him," Holly said. "It couldn't be."

"She had a change of heart once she cooled off," Josh persisted. "Especially when she started to get overdraft notices from the bank because the direct deposits from his paychecks had stopped, and she discovered he'd cleaned out their safe-deposit box and cashed in their stocks. Then she called his boss and found out he'd quit showing up for work. That's when she called the cops. It has all the earmarks of a voluntary departure. No laws have been broken, but she insists something's happened to him, that he wouldn't trash his job and abandon his wife and kiddies."

"Children?" Holly asked.

"Two daughters," Josh said.

Holly shivered. "I don't believe it." She met Craig's eyes. "I could believe that you're married. And maybe even that you have children. But not that you would get drunk, flirt in front of your wife and then give her a black eye when she complained."

Josh scowled. "For God's sake, Holly! You're an intelligent woman. What does it take to make you see the truth?"

"More than a piece of paper!" she said.

"A piece of paper with a description of lover boy here, right down to the scar."

Holly looked at Craig. "You're not six-three, are you?"

"Six one and a half," Craig said. "They measured at the hospital."

Josh shrugged. "Men exaggerate. If this guy told his wife he was six-three, she wouldn't question it."

"You want it to be him!" Holly accused.

"Damn it, Holly! Quit blaming me. I don't like seeing you get hurt. But I can't ignore the truth when it bites me on the butt."

"You wouldn't *recognize* the truth if it did bite you on the butt!" she retorted.

Josh vented his frustration in a sigh. "I'm only the messenger, honey. You're the one who asked me to check into things. I didn't make up the report."

"He's right, Holly," Craig said. "He's only doing his job. You can't blame him for what he finds out."

"Actually, it's my job," Scalisi said. "And until we get a callback on the fax, I have to agree with the lady. All we have is a piece of paper." He pinned Craig with an interrogative scowl. "Unless you suddenly remember something."

Craig shook his head.

"The name Thomas Martin McClure doesn't sound familiar at all?"

Another shake of the head.

"The names Amanda McClure, Jennifer McClure or Elizabeth McClure?"

"No!" Craig said. "No. I don't recognize any of them."

"In that case," Scalisi said, "I suggest we all go back to work until we hear whether your picture rings any bells with Mrs. McClure."

"When do you expect to hear?" Holly asked.

"Could be any time," Scalisi said. "We'll let you know the minute I find out."

"Josh?" Holly said when the two cops moved to leave.

He turned to look at her.

"Thanks for your help," she said.

He grinned affably and bobbed his chin, then followed Scalisi out of the room, closing the door, leaving Craig and Holly alone.

The familiar room suddenly seemed too quiet. Holding her hands in his, Craig rose, and urged her to do the same, guiding her into his arms as she got up. "I need to hold you."

"Just try to pry me away!" she replied, pressing her face into his chest, noting at once his hard strength, his warmth and the scent of him, faintly musky and distinctively male.

"You're trembling," he said.

"So are you."

"I was so sure," he said. "So certain that I was incapable of forgetting a wife and children, so sure that I wasn't being unfair to you."

"You've never lied to me," she said, quieting him by lifting her fingers to his mouth. "I've known about the question marks from the beginning."

"I just assumed that even without memories, I would know myself, what kind of person I am. But if it's true, if I'm Thomas Martin McClure, if I left my wife and kids destitute, if I'm a wife beater—"

"You're not."

His eyes searched her face for a long moment. "You have more faith in me than I have in myself."

"I've never seen you drink anything but very good wine, and then only responsibly. Now, if the story was that you ate too much ice cream and hit your wife in a sugar-induced psychotic state—"

She'd succeeded in making him smile. "I *have* been consuming a lot of ice cream lately."

"I'm considering buying stock in the dairy." They'd spent every nonworking hour together in the week and a half since the Big Bad Wolf had appeared at her door. They'd picnicked in the park, watched countless movies, talked for hours on end and made love every chance they got.

Craig was into his fifth half-gallon carton of ice cream.

"Do you want to take the rest of the day off?" she asked. "I'm sure if we asked—"

"We've only got another hour before closing," he said. "I'd rather stay busy, anyway."

Nodding, she took a step back, but he stopped her retreat by wrapping his hands loosely around her arms. "Holly?"

Her eyes met his questioningly.

"No matter what happens—"

After several beats of silence, she nodded.

"God!" he said, flinging his arms around her.

He held her next to him for a very long time before letting her go with no words spoken, but with volumes understood between them.

After work, they rode most of the way to her apartment in thoughtful silence. Finally, Craig said, "How long would it take her to look at a photo?"

Holly shrugged. "It's probably more a case of how long it takes the cops in Virginia to get around to showing it to her."

At her apartment, Holly changed into comfortable clothes, then joined Craig in the living room, where he was reading the newspaper. He put it down when he heard her enter the room and patted the cushion next to him. She plopped down with a prolonged sigh and relaxed against him with her head on his shoulder. "The pool's still open. Want to go swim off some stress?"

"No."

"Want to watch the news?"

"Uh-uh."

"Hungry?"

"No."

"Want to just sit here and pretend the rest of the world doesn't exist?"

"For as long as we can get away with it."

For a quarter of an hour, Holly listened to the beat of his heart and tried to pretend, but the world wouldn't go away. They'd been pretending for weeks, and now reality was stalking them. The phone was going to ring or there would be a knock at the door. The best they could hope for was a longer stint in limbo.

Holly didn't want to think about the alternative. She didn't want to imagine him backhanding a woman he was supposed to love. She just wanted to listen to his heart and believe that he was the gentle man she had come to care about. And that he could be hers.

"I don't want to lose you, Holly."

If he hadn't lifted her hand and pressed the back of it to his cheek just then, she might have wondered if he'd really spoken.

"No matter what happens, I want *us*," he continued.

He was kissing her fingers, and she felt it all the way to her womb. "Why don't we wait until we—"

He cut her off. "I'm in love with you."

Holly squeezed her eyes shut and snuggled closer as he nibbled on her pinkie. The words were in her throat to tell him that she loved him, too, when the doorbell rang, shattering the mood.

Shocked, they sprang to attention. Craig exhaled a moan of frustration. She was already getting up, but he was still holding her hand. "Holly—"

"We have to hear it, whatever it is." With effort, she smiled at him reassuringly.

With a desolate nod of agreement, he let go of her hand. She walked slowly to the door, wondering if anything would ever be the same after she answered it.

Josh was almost obscenely cheerful as he bounded into the apartment and announced, "Well, kiddies, I have bad news and I have good news. Which do you want first?"

"Just tell us what you found out," Holly said, trying to remember that Josh had no way of knowing how poorly timed his arrival had been.

"The good news first, then." Tilting his head toward Craig, he said, "You, sir, are not Thomas Martin McClure, wife beater and family deserter."

"Mrs. McClure saw his picture?" Holly asked.

"In her words, quoted directly from the authorities in Virginia, 'In my wildest dreams, Thomas would look like that.'"

Holly exhaled the breath she'd been holding. "And the bad news?" she asked hoarsely.

"We're back to square one," Josh answered. "We still don't know who the hell he is."

Holly's eyes met Craig's jubilantly. Square one wasn't such a bad place to be!

After an indeterminate silence, Josh shuffled restlessly. "Oh, for— Why don't you two kiss and get it over with."

As far as Craig was concerned, the suggestion was superfluous. If the building had been on fire, he'd have taken the time to kiss Holly before carrying her out. The strength of her embrace and the ardor of her kiss telegraphed the same sense of relief. He continued holding her after the kiss ended, keeping his arm draped securely across her shoulders. "Thanks for letting us know," he told Josh.

Josh shrugged. "Anything for a friend."

"What's in the bag?" Holly asked, pointing to a plastic supermarket bag dangling from his right hand.

"A peace offering. I thought we'd celebrate."

"You thought I'd cook dinner," Holly corrected.

Wincing, Josh groaned playfully. "Come on, Holly. You know no one can make shrimp the way you do." He looked at Craig. "Holly *has* made you her special garlic shrimp, hasn't she?"

"I haven't had the pleasure yet," Craig said.

"Then get ready for a taste that would make the gods weep with ecstasy."

"I'm being cajoled," Holly said, but the protest fell on unresponsive ears.

"I brought French bread and shrimp and real butter and fresh garlic and romaine lettuce and red potatoes," Josh said. Then, turning to Craig, he added, "She makes these potatoes to go with the shrimp that...well, I can't even describe them, except to say—" He made a circle of his thumb and forefinger and kissed it.

"You need to find yourself a woman," Holly said. "One who can cook."

"You're the last woman on earth who enjoys cooking," Josh said. "You're the only woman I've ever met who doesn't think potatoes grow in supermarket freezers or foil pouches. And your shrimp—"

"You two are going to do the dishes!" Holly said.

"Deal!" Josh said. "We'll even keep you company in the kitchen while you cook."

"You guys are all heart," Holly said, taking the bag and poking into it. "I hope these shrimp are fresh."

"If they were any fresher, they'd have swam in the door," Josh said.

An hour later, the table was set, the Caesar salad tossed, the potatoes simmering. Josh and Craig stood near the range watching the shrimp sauté under Holly's careful supervision.

Josh sucked in a lungful of air scented with the blend of garlic and butter. "It's miraculous," he said. "Those smelly little shrimp transformed into this."

"Exactly how long *has* it been since you had a home-cooked meal?" Holly asked, picking up a bottle of crushed red pepper.

"Easter," he replied. "Ham, green beans and candied yams. My new partner's mother insisted."

Holly eyed the bottle of pepper, then looked at Craig. "Do you mind? This is pretty hot."

"Go for it!" he said. "I like my food spicy." He grinned and gave his eyebrows a lecherous lift. "Just like my women."

The pall that followed was no normal silence, and the shocked looks that passed between Holly and Josh unsettled Craig. He had committed some sort of gaffe, but what? Holly surely knew he was teasing. She usually found his flirtatious comments amusing.

"What did I say?" he asked.

Again, Holly and Josh exchanged mysterious looks before Holly turned her attention back to sprinkling pepper over the shrimp, leaving the question for Josh to answer.

"Someone we knew used to say that," he said.

"What?" Craig asked.

"I like my food spicy—just like my women," Josh replied.

Holly's fiancé, of course. "I'm sorry, Holly. I didn't mean to—"

"It's just a silly expression," Holly said, turning the shrimp.

"Strange coincidence," Craig said.

"The shrimp are done," Holly said, and they adjourned to the table.

Josh left after helping with the dishes. When he'd gone, Holly chained the door then leaned against it.

Craig was standing a few feet away, and as she discovered him staring at her, their earlier conversation came rushing back as though it had never been interrupted.

She walked over and draped her arms over his shoulders. "You were saying?"

He told her again that he loved her, using touch instead of words. His hands were gentle on her body, his lips tender on hers. The sweetness of the kiss was shattering, the serenity she felt as he held her afterward precious.

He cradled her face. "I have so much to tell you. And I want to be able to see your face when I do." He guided her to the armchair, and urged her into his lap. Holly was struck by the overall rightness about being there with him, the comfortable intimacy between them as his hand rested warmly on her ribs.

They had a lot to talk about but, for a long while, he seemed content just to look at her face, smiling gently. Then he said, "I have a confession to make."

Holly tensed. "Confession?" *Please don't tell me you've been deceiving me that you're a deadbeat or a con man. Don't tell me that everything I believe about you is a lie.*

"You're the reason I went to work at the library," he said.

"I don't understand—how could that be?"

"The first day I moved into my apartment, I was out walking, and saw the library. I went in and read some magazines and wandered around. It must have been a Thursday, because you were in the middle of Story Hour, and you . . ." He smiled. "I heard the kids laughing, and looked over and . . . there you were, reading, and the kids were hanging on to every word."

She was aware of a subtle change in the way he was holding her, an almost imperceptible tightening of his embrace as he continued, "I stood there watching you and I couldn't imagine anything more beautiful than your face. I still can't."

"I'm not beautiful," Holly said. Wholesome, yes. Pleasing, yes. But she wasn't a woman who turned heads or stopped traffic.

"It's not just your features, Holly. It's...what comes from within—generosity and sensitivity and kindness. When I saw you with the children, something just clicked."

"I must resemble someone you know, someone you care about."

"I thought so at first," he said, and laughed softly. "Especially when I started dreaming about you at night."

"The fact that you reacted to me interacting with children—"

"It doesn't mean that I have children," he said. "I see kids and think they're cute and sweet, but I don't feel . . . *paternal*. A man with kids would feel . . . like a daddy."

"And what does a daddy feel like?"

"I don't know!" he said. "That's just the point."

"Maybe you don't feel married because you can't remember your wife." Suddenly, her fears came pouring out, one after the other. "Maybe you don't feel like someone's daddy because you can't remember your children. Maybe missing them would hurt too much if you retained the feelings, so some internal defense mechanism has clicked in to protect you. Maybe you cling to me because—"

"I cling to you because from the first time I saw you, there was a connection. Call it chemistry, or predestination—" He shook his head. "I just know that when I saw the library job on the list at the employment office, my first thought was that if I went to work there, I would get to meet you. And that the first time you noticed me, the first time I looked into your eyes—"

He laughed softly. "It sounds corny, doesn't it? Like the lyrics to a sentimental old song. But when it happens . . ." He brushed her hair away from her face with his fingertips and gazed into her eyes. "The love I feel for you is real, Holly. It's the genuine article. It may be the only thing in my life that is real right now. And I need to know—" He exhaled a sigh of frustration. "I have no right . . . nothing to offer you. But I love you, and nothing is going to change that."

He waited for Holly to respond. And waited. Finally, unable to stand the suspense, he prompted impatiently, "I just bared my soul to you. Do you think you could say something? Anything?"

Her gentle smile etched his heart as she combed her fingers into his hair. "What makes you think you have nothing to offer me?"

He thought it would have been obvious. "I have no past, and God only knows what kind of future. That's not much to lay at a woman's feet."

"The past is like a match that's already been struck," she said. "And the future...no one owns the future. It's not ours until it becomes the present." Her fingers curved over his nape, soothing as only a woman's touch could soothe. "If I learned anything from Craig's death, it's that right now is all anyone really has. And in the end, the only thing that counts is the love you give. Or receive."

Craig pondered what she'd said, then with an impatient sniff, said, "Help me out here, Holly. Is there a snowball's chance in hell that you love me half as much as I love you?"

"Half as much?" she asked, leaning forward until her breasts crushed against his chest and her mouth was scarcely an inch from his. "You underestimate me."

9

FOR SEVERAL DAYS following the false alarm regarding Craig's identity, Holly and Craig were spared any new reminders of the precariousness of Craig's situation. Like honeymooners, self-absorbed and oblivious to the world around them, they avoided talking about the unanswered questions that shadowed their future. By unspoken mutual agreement, they ignored what they could not change and refused to dwell on uncertainties.

Madly in love, Holly told herself that the questions didn't matter, and most of the time it was easy to let herself believe it. When she was with him, the rest of the world seemed far away, and when he held her, the question marks seemed less menacing. But there were times when the reality of their situation refused to be ignored, when she was forced to think about the mysteries surrounding the man with whom she'd fallen in love.

One such time came in the middle of the night, five days after the false alarm, when she awoke to Craig's anguished screams. Crying his name, she grasped his upper arm and shook him, but he fought her, lashing out blindly in his sleep. "Craig!" she called again, firmly, almost shouting.

His eyes sprang open and the horrific groans that had awakened Holly faded into labored breathing. "Wha—

Holly?" He folded her into his arms, drawing her hard against him.

"You were having a nightmare," she said, relaxing a bit as she felt his breathing return to normal.

"It seemed so real," he said.

"Tell me about it."

"Something happened. My chest . . . hurt. It was like something had exploded inside it. And I looked down and saw that I was bleeding. I put my hands over the wound and tried to stop the blood, but I couldn't. And I thought, 'I'm dying.'"

He shuddered. Holly pressed a reassuring kiss on his neck. "It's over now. You're safe."

"I think . . . Holly, I think it was more than a dream. You've seen the scar on my chest—I must have been re-living the past."

"Do you remember any details? How it happened?"

He shook his head. "Only the pain. And the blood. And thinking that I was dying."

"Too bad," Holly said, snuggling closer and yawning.

"Yeah," he said bitterly. "Too bad I didn't have the presence of mind to recall my name while I was dreaming down memory lane."

Holly tried to go back to sleep, but Craig was restless, and she found herself unable to relax when he was so tense. "Did you really dream about me before we met?" she asked.

"Yes. And afterward."

"What did you dream?"

A subtle shift of his cheek against her temple told her he was smiling.

"The kinds of wild, erotic things adolescent boys dream about cheerleaders."

"I'm serious."

"So am I."

Holly shifted and exhaled a sigh that fell short of expressing irritation.

Craig pressed his thigh closer to hers. "I'll tell you about one of the most vivid. You were at the beach. Your hair was longer and you had it pulled up in two ponytails. You were wearing a two-piece swimsuit. Bright pink. It was so hot, I couldn't keep my eyes off you."

He paused to take a breath, then continued, "We were with a big group of people. We were playing volleyball, men against the women. It was a grudge match, and both teams were jeering and taunting each other, but I wasn't thinking about the game."

There was something vaguely disturbing about the way he related the details of the dream, making it sound so real. There was also something hauntingly familiar about the scenario he described.

"One of the guys volleyed right to you, just over your head, and you jumped for it. And when you jumped, the top of your swimsuit popped up. The guys all started hooting and acting like jackasses. You were mortified, of course. You covered yourself with your hands and all the women closed ranks around you to shield you while you pulled your top back on."

His breath fanned through her hair. "It was only a glimpse, but I saw your breasts, and they were creamy and white, and the nipples were a light, rosy brown, and all I could think about was how much I wanted to touch you there. Some fantasy, huh? Although I much prefer reality."

Holly lay very still as he covered her breasts with his hands and kneaded them. *No*, she thought. *It wasn't a fantasy at all.*

Sensing her unnatural stillness, he said, "I didn't offend you, did I?"

"No!" Holly said, thinking fiercely, *You terrified me!*

"Holly?"

"Kiss me," she said, turning her face toward his. "Please. Just . . . kiss me."

When he kissed her, everything was all right.

When he made love to her, the world went away.

When they were together, the question marks didn't matter.

"YOU WANT TO KNOW what happened when Craig was shot?"

Holly nodded.

"Why are you suddenly curious about this?" Josh asked.

"I'm letting go," Holly said. "Maybe I've just reached the point where I can stand to hear it."

"Nice try," Josh said. "But I don't believe a word of it."

"What do you mean?" Holly said, feigning innocence. She should have known she couldn't put anything past Josh. He was too detail-oriented, and she was lousy at bluffing.

"What do I mean?" Josh mimicked. "You call me over for a clandestine meeting—"

"Clandestine? At my apartment, in the middle of the day?"

"On the only day that your boyfriend works and you don't."

"I just didn't think he needed to hear us talk about Craig. It doesn't have anything to do with him," Holly lied.

Josh frowned skeptically before asking, "What do want to know?"

"When he—" She paused and started over. This was even harder than she'd thought it would be. "When he was . . . hit, how did he—did he know it? Did he realize what had happened? Did he say anything, or do anything?" She looked Josh fully in the face. "You were there, Josh. Please tell me. The smallest details. It's important."

Josh's shoulders slumped. The memory of the day his partner was killed weighted his features. Words did not come easily. Finally, he said, "We heard the shot, and then Craig looked down at his chest and saw blood. He seemed . . . surprised."

Josh swallowed. "Are you sure you want to hear this?"

Holly studied her hands. "Yes."

"It's not going to serve any purpose."

"I need to know."

Josh nodded. "He made a sound. It wasn't really a word, just a sound, like a wounded animal. And he put his hands over the wound, as though he could stop the blood from coming out, and he looked at me, as if to say, 'I can't make it stop.'"

"I looked down and saw that I was bleeding. I put my hands over the wound and tried to stop the blood, but I couldn't."

"The creep went to shoot again, but his gun misfired, and that's when I rushed him and wrestled him to the ground. By the time I had him cuffed, our backup had arrived and they were calling for an ambulance. I went over to Craig, and he looked up at me. I swear to God, Holly, I'll never forget what he said. He said, 'I'm dying.' Just like that. Just like he'd have said that his nose itched."

"And I thought, 'I'm dying.'"

"I tried to reassure him, but by the time the ambulance got there, he'd lost consciousness."

Holly felt the damp heat of tears running down her cheeks. "Thank you for telling me."

"What's this really about, Holly?"

"I just—"

Josh lifted a book from the coffee table and held it up. "Does it have anything to do with this?"

The title of the book stood out in raised gold letters on a red background to mock her: *The Mystery of Reincarnation.* "You had no right to spy on me," she said.

"It's hardly spying," Josh replied. "The book was on the table in plain sight."

"Facedown."

"Why?"

Holly's lips compressed in irritation.

"Why are you asking about Craig now, why are you reading about reincarnation and why would you deliberately lay the book on the table facedown so I wouldn't see what you were reading about?"

"Because—" She sighed as if she'd been saddled with the cares of the entire world. "If I told you, you'd think I've come unhinged."

"Try me," he said.

She remained steadfastly silent.

"Look, Holly, I know you think I'm a jerk sometimes, but Craig was my best friend, and he loved you, and that makes me feel just a little responsible for you. You called me for help when you wanted your boyfriend checked out, and you called me today to ask me about Craig. Why don't you try confiding in me? I might surprise you with my sensitivity."

"Right!" she said with a grudging grin.

"If you could confide in that boyfriend of yours, you would."

"You've got to promise to hear me out. No matter how crazy it sounds," she said.

"I'm a cop, Holly. You're not going to shock me."

She exhaled heavily. "Last week, when I was putting pepper on the shrimp and Craig said that he liked his food spicy, just like his women—it sounded like—"

"Craig," Josh said. "The real Craig. I don't mind telling you, Holly, it gives me the creeps when you call this guy Craig. It seems blasphemous."

"They don't retire names like team jerseys," Holly said. "Craig doesn't have a monopoly on the name just because he died."

"If this guy had been named after his grandfather and had a mother who still called him Craiggy-Pooh, it wouldn't bother me. It's knowing that he just picked it out of the air that bothers me. But we're off the subject."

"That comment wasn't the first . . . coincidence," Holly said.

"What kind of coincidences are we talking about here?"

"It wasn't the first time he's used one of Craig's phrases. And—this is—sort of personal, but Craig—the original Craig—always craved ice cream after—you know, we were together."

"Smokers want a cigarette, but Craig wanted chocolate chip with mint."

Her eyes registered surprise. "You knew about the ice cream?"

"Craig was no virgin when he met you, Holly. There had been other women. The guys knew about his ice-cream fetish. They used to tease him when he'd start dating a new woman, asking if he was going to have ice cream for dessert."

"Everyone knew?" The idea appalled her.

"Hell, Holly. That's how we knew he was serious about you. When he said he was going to be dipping from the same carton for the rest of his life, we knew he was a goner."

Fresh tears burned Holly's eyes. It was so quintessentially Craig, so romantic in a tough guy-cop kind of way.

"Don't you think it's odd that Craig—the new Craig—would like ice cream, too?"

"This is why you're reading books on reincarnation?" Josh asked incredulously. *"Ice cream after sex?"*

"It's more than that," Holly said. "It's phrases that he uses, and he dipped me after we danced—"

"Another coincidence. A lot of people do that."

"Buttercup plays with him the same way she played with Craig. She growls and swats his finger with her paws."

"That cat of yours would play with anyone who'd play back."

"She doesn't play with you," Holly said. "She doesn't come near you."

"She knows I can't stand cats," Josh said.

Holly leveled her gaze on his. "He dreamed Craig's memories."

"Whoa!" Josh said. "Back up. He *dreams* Craig's memories?"

"I told you it was going to sound crazy."

Josh wiped his hand over his face. "You're damned right. But go on."

"Two nights ago, he woke up in the middle of a nightmare. He thought he was remembering when he was hurt. He has a scar—"

"On his chest, extending to his shoulder. That's on the MP reports."

"He thought he was remembering when *he* got hurt. But it—it just didn't click. When he was telling me about it— But I still didn't believe—" She sighed. "And then he told me about another dream, a dream he'd had about me. He called it an adolescent fantasy."

"So?"

"It was the beach party, Josh. The one Craig took me to when we first met. Remember, when I jumped for the ball and my swimsuit—"

"Remember?" Josh said, with a chortle. "Holly, you're a legend down at the station."

Holly buried her face in her hands, and a shudder wracked her shoulders. "He dreamed it as though he'd been there. He described the way I had my hair, the swimsuit I wore, and the . . . what happened at the volleyball game. He said things that Craig said to me afterward."

"It was so hot I couldn't keep my eyes off you."

She went on, "He used words that Craig—"

"The real Craig," Josh interjected.

"Your friend Craig," Holly corrected. "Josh, he called my breasts creamy."

"And all I could think about was how much I wanted to touch you there."

Josh hooted. "That's it? Hell, Holly, there's nothing mysterious about that. Every man there thought your breasts were creamy."

"But he wasn't there!" Holly said. "Craig—the man you knew—was there, but not the man who was in my bed two nights ago telling me about his dream." Her composure cracked, and a desperate sob tore from her throat. "How could he dream someone else's memories, Josh?"

"He couldn't," Josh said.

"But he did!" Holly said, near hysteria. "And he—" She swallowed a sob. "He thought he was remembering when he was hurt, when he got the scar on his chest, but it was more like when Craig was shot. He described it bit by bit exactly the way you did—looking down at the blood, trying to stop it, realizing he was dying."

"What are you suggesting, Holly? That Craig has come back from the dead, taller and prettier, but just as horny?"

"I don't know," she said, desperate, almost shouting. "At first, I thought it was just coincidence. The name, a random word, a turn of phrase—ice cream after sex. I tried to explain them away one by one. But suddenly there were too many, and I realized that there had been something about him all along, something that attracted me to him."

"It's called chemistry. Also known as raging hormones."

"It was more than that. Craig felt it, too. He was sure we'd met and I wasn't telling him. He said he knew all about me, what it would be like to—"

Josh sprang from the couch. "He's not Craig!" he said, driving his hand through his hair. "Craig's dead. He's gone, and he's not coming back."

He paced the narrow room like a caged animal until, finally, he stopped and glared at her. "For God's sake— or for Craig's memory's sake—would you use that pretty little head on your shoulders for something besides a hat rack? This man isn't Craig, conveniently reincarnated into James Bond minus the English accent. From what you've just told me, he sounds like a very clever con man."

Holly's chin quivered. "He's not a con man. He can't be." *I love him.*

Josh knelt next to her chair and lifted her hands. "Honey, I know there's nothing you'd like more than for Craig to come back. I wish he could come back, too. But he's gone, and someone is playing a cruel trick on you, playing with your emotions."

"How? Why? Josh, what would he have to gain?"

"To start with, he's in your bed."

"We've had this conversation before," Holly said. "A man like Craig wouldn't have to go to much trouble to get a woman into his bed. I'm not beautiful, and I'm certainly not wealthy. Why would he target me?"

"Maybe you don't see it so much in the kiddy section of the public library, but the world is full of weirdos," Josh said. "He could be someone Craig busted, or the brother of someone Craig busted, or the brother of some girl who thinks Craig broke her heart and sees you as the reason."

"Get real!" Holly said.

"It makes a hell of a lot more sense than your cockamamy reincarnation theory! Don't you go to the movies? Didn't you see *Fatal Attraction* or *Play Misty For Me?* Hell hath no fury like a woman scorned. We arrested a woman last week who broke into her exboyfriend's new girlfriend's house and left a snake in her underwear drawer."

"I might have believed it when Craig—the first Craig—and I first started dating, or when we became engaged, but Craig's been dead a year. How sick would someone have to be to want to punish me after I lost him?"

"Someone who blames you for his death."

"Blames me? I didn't have anything to do with his getting killed."

"Anyone with a lick of sense knows that," Josh said. "But no one with a lick of sense would plan something this twisted in the first place."

Holly tried to imagine the scenario he proposed. She tried to envision Craig practicing lines and memorizing details. She tried to open her mind to the possibility that he was deliberately deceiving her. But she could not. She saw instead a sensitive man with haunted eyes, a gentle, thoughtful man with an endearing sense of humor and a beautiful smile. Deliberately hurt her? He was incapable of it.

"He's not a con man," she said.

"You're sure?"

She nodded. Josh rolled his eyes. "Deliver me from women's intuition!"

Long seconds passed before Holly said softly, "I'm in love with him."

"I figured as much."

"Must be that cop's intuition of yours."

"I didn't need intuition. All I had to do was open my eyes. You two look at each other like lovesick spaniels."

"That's what I've always loved about you, Josh. Your poetic soul."

"Give me a break! I haven't had a date in six months, and that one was a dud. Do you think it's easy watching my best friend's girl play goo-goo, patty-cake with a con artist?"

"*Alleged* con artist. If you're going to put everything into cop terminology, at least get it right."

Josh harrumphed skeptically.

"He *is* innocent until proven guilty, you know," she said.

Josh sighed. "I have given this guy the benefit of every doubt possible, Holly, reasonable and otherwise. I have tried to take his story at face value. I've tried to be nice to him. Hell, I even *like* him. But being likable is the stock and trade of con men. And after what you've told me tonight, I can't ignore the coincidences."

Holly glared at him.

"Don't look at me like that!" he said. "You can't afford to ignore them, either. At least be prepared for the possibility that he's playing you in a cruel and vicious way."

Holly was still glaring at him. Finally, he exhaled wearily. "For your sake," he said, "I hope this guy's on the level. But I'm going to be on him like a duck on a june bug. If he's running a scam, he's going to wish he could lose the memory of what happens next. And Holly—"

She looked at him expectantly.

"Get rid of the book and forget this reincarnation nonsense. Either he's scamming you, and you're convinced he's not, or he just likes ice cream."

"And the dreams?"

He shrugged. "You tell me. Maybe he was on the beach that day and saw the whole thing. Or maybe it *was* just a fantasy. There's never been a man alive who could look at a woman in a swimsuit and not wish something would either pop out or fall down."

"Josh! I never realized what a romantic you are!"

"I'll tell you how romantic I am," he said. "If I find out your boy is perpetrating a scam, I'm going to hang him from a flagpole and mail you his ears."

"And if you find out who he really is, and he turns out to be a perfectly respectable insurance salesman from Ohio . . . ?"

"Then I'll deejay at your wedding reception for free," he said. He chortled and shook his head in incredulity. "Maybe I really am a bit of a romantic. Believe it or not, for your sake, I sorta hope it works out that way."

10

CRAIG LEANED across the seat to give Holly a brief hello kiss. "How was your day?"

"Nice and lazy," she replied, deciding that the innocuous lie was harmless enough. She could hardly tell him that she'd spent her day off assuring Josh that Craig wasn't a con artist and reading about reincarnation because he'd dreamed a beach party she'd gone to years earlier with another man.

She'd spent the hours following Josh's visit pondering how complicated her life had become. She was a small-town librarian. Small-town librarians weren't supposed to fall in love with men shrouded in unknowns. Nor were they supposed to spend their days off reading books on reincarnation, fruitlessly searching for answers to riddles that had perplexed philosophers and theologians for centuries.

She'd dropped the book in the library's night depository on her way into the building to meet Craig. Now she was left with the dilemma of whether or not to tell him about Josh's suspicions—or her own.

"I was thinking that a walk along the beach might be nice," she suggested impulsively. "If you're not too tired."

"I'm never too tired for a walk on the beach with you," he said.

The night mimicked Holly's mood. Cloud-shrouded stars and a quarter moon cast only a faint light, and a brisk wind whipped at their hair and clothing. Hand in hand, they followed the tide line for several hundred yards before turning around to retrace their steps. Holly stopped and turned to face the ocean. The churning seawater appeared murky and endless and disappeared into a blue-black void in the distance.

"On nights like this, it's easy to see why people used to think they'd fall off the edge of the earth if they went too far offshore," she said.

"Sometimes I feel just that way about my past," he said, staring into the distance. "Like it's a great, dark emptiness just waiting to swallow me up."

"What scares you most?" she asked softly.

Turning to her, he raised his hands to cradle her face. In the faint light, she could see only the shadow of the smile lifting the corners of his mouth, and the warm glow of adoration in his eyes. "The possibility of losing you."

She stepped closer to him and he wrapped his arms around her, holding her tight. Sighing, she rested her cheek against his chest. "I'm not that easy to lose," she said. "The last man I loved died and I didn't stop loving him."

"I may not be the person you love, the person I like to believe I am. I could be so . . . *evil*, or *immoral* that my mind chose to blot out the person I am rather than live with the truth."

"Didn't the doctors say that your memory loss was consistent with the head injury you had, that it was physical, rather than psychological?"

"I just can't shake the fear that I'll finally remember, and that what I remember will be something *horrible*." A shudder wracked his shoulders. "If I ran in front of that car deliberately—"

His arms tightened around her convulsively. "No one anywhere seems to care enough about me to look for me, and this wound on my shoulder could be anything—a gunshot, a stabbing. I could be a criminal. A hit man for the mob. I could have been a spy, what they call an operative. I could have been given a drug of some kind to eradicate my memory."

Holly snuggled her cheek over his heart. "Whoever you are, you've seen too many movies, and you have a fertile imagination."

And maybe she did, too. Books on reincarnation, indeed!

They held each other for a very long time before Craig said, "Every time I hold you, I'm afraid that if I let you go, I might never hold you again."

Then hold me, she thought fiercely. *Hold me and never let me go*. "We have now," she said. "We'll make the most of it."

FOR FIVE DAYS, "now" remained an enchanted place. Holly loved Craig with an intensity and fierceness that shut out the world with all its vagaries and unknowns. Craig returned her love with the same ardor. He never kissed her without telling her that he loved her; he never hugged her without a verbal assurance that no matter what happened, they would find a way for things to work out.

Although they avoided talking about the uncertainties that hung over their relationship like the savage pendulum suspended over the pit in her heart, Holly knew that eventually, inevitably, Craig's past would insinuate itself into their relationship. She saw her own fear reflected in Craig's eyes, and sensed desperation in the way he touched her—the same desperation that made her cling to him with every embrace.

Saturday after work, they changed into comfortable clothes, called for a pizza and settled in to watch the movies Holly had checked out from the library's video collection. The evening stretched ahead of them filled with the promise of pleasure.

"This first movie is really sad," Holly said, hitting the play button. "We may need tissues."

"I thought you didn't like sad movies," Craig said.

"This one's an exception." She cuddled close to Craig, resting her head on his shoulder and stretching her arm across his waist in front.

The film flashed onto the screen. "What is this?" Craig protested. "A cartoon? Pepe Le Pew? I thought you said it was a sad movie!"

"Pepe never gets the girl," she said.

"He's a skunk!"

"Nobody's perfect," Holly said with laughter in her voice. "Skunks need affection like anybody else."

"Saturday night and we're watching a skunk try to seduce a cat!" Craig grumbled good-naturedly.

"Are you complaining about the quality of the entertainment?" Holly teased.

With an unexpected but deft maneuver, he pushed her back onto the couch and crouched over her. "*Chérie*, do you not know that there ees nowhere else on earth I'd rather be than with you?" he said in a perfect imitation of Pepe. "*Tu es jolie. Tu es sexy. Je t'aime avec touts mon coeur. Viens avec moi au Casbah et fais l'amour avec moi."*

"You speak French?"

"Mais oui, chérie. C'est la langue d'amour."

"You speak French!" she repeated.

He chortled, as shocked as she. "I'll be damned. I speak French." He absorbed the information for several seconds before giving her a deliberately lecherous look. "Now, where were we, *ma petite chou?* Ah, yes—*l'amour!"*

With a mock-savage growl, he pretended to take a bite from her neck, then, lifting his head, he kissed his fingertips and released an exaggerated sigh. *"Tu es—"*

The doorbell rang. *"Je suis...*going to get the pizza," Holly said, pushing on his chest with the flat of her hands.

"Mais, chérie—who needs food when we have each other?"

"Man does not live on *l'amour* alone," she said. "Nor does woman."

"We could try," he said.

Holly picked up the money they'd put on the table in anticipation of the pizza delivery and, cash in hand, opened the door to greet the deliveryman. Everything inside her went cold with premonition when she discovered who had really rung the bell: Josh.

Spying Craig approaching, he said, "Oh, good. You're both here. I thought you'd want to hear the good news together."

"Good news?" Craig asked. He draped his arm across Holly's shoulders as Josh stepped into the room.

"I waited until we were sure this time," Josh said.

"You know who I am?" Holly felt Craig tense as he asked the question.

"Do you two want to sit down to hear this?"

"Just tell us," Craig snapped.

Josh shrugged. "All right. Here it is. Your name is Timothy Edward Sotherland, and you're an architect from Cincinnati."

"Timothy Edward Sotherland," Craig repeated. His face took on a sudden pallor, but Holly assumed that was to be expected.

"The reason no one filed a report on you is that you were supposed to be touring Europe on an extended sabbatical. Soaking up inspiration from old-world architecture or something. Apparently, you're a very promising young architect, because you won a pretty important design competition with a substantial cash endowment."

"The VonFremdam Memorial Grant."

"You remember?" Josh asked. He didn't seem to notice the odd flatness in Craig's voice.

Timothy Sotherland's voice, Holly corrected in her mind.

"Yes. I . . . when you said my name—"

He crumbled so suddenly that neither of them had time to react. Holly grabbed for his arm, but her strength was no match for his weight and the downward momentum he'd already gathered. Josh had lunged to catch him, but was half a second too late to do any good.

Craig's head hit the corner of an end table with a sickening thunk. A groan pushed its way through his throat as his head rolled limply to the side.

"Craig!" Holly dropped to her knees beside him and gasped in horror at the puddle of blood gathering beneath his head. Instinctively, she reached to check the injury, but Josh, also kneeling, clasped her wrist.

"Don't move him. If he's sustained a neck- or spinal-cord injury, you could make it worse."

"Call an ambulance!" she ordered.

"You got it!"

Holly was only vaguely aware of his using the phone before he returned with a towel, which he carefully tucked near Craig's head. "This should protect your carpet a little."

"Who cares about the carpet?" she snapped at him. "Craig could be dying!"

"Tim," Josh corrected. "And I don't think he's dying. He hit on the toughest part of his head."

"But the blood—"

"A little blood goes a long way," Josh said.

"I hope you're right," she said, staring at the stain dubiously. "What's keeping the ambulance?"

"It's only been two minutes."

"It seems like forever."

Seconds continued to crawl snaillike into what seemed like hours. The paramedics arrived, strapped Craig to a board and started an IV line. "His pulse is strong and his breathing is normal," one of the paramedics told her. "It's probably not too bad."

All Holly could do was nod gratefully and trail after them as they wheeled Craig out to the ambulance, then watch as they loaded the gurney onto the vehicle.

Josh drove her to the hospital behind the ambulance. "He's going to be just fine," he said. "You heard the paramedic. They don't hand out false optimism."

Hands balled into tight fists, Holly stared at the blinking lights of the vehicle ahead of them, imagining Craig, pale and still, strapped and wired, inside. Craig Ford. *Timothy Sotherland.* An architect.

"He's not married," Josh said.

"What?" Holly said. Her mind teemed with questions, but her concern for his welfare superseded them.

"He's single. Never been married."

"One thing at a time," she said. "I'll celebrate his bachelorhood as soon as I know he's going to be all right."

He was all right. He had to be. She repeated the litany over and over to herself during the endless wait for news at the hospital.

SOMEONE WAS POKING needles into the side of his head. Was the groan he heard his own?

"He's coming around," said a female voice.

"Wh-what?" Tim asked, but the word didn't sound right. He tried to open his eyes, then shut them against the piercing light.

A soothing hand stroked his upper arm, and the voice said, "Just relax and lie still. You're in the emergency room. You've had a bump on the head. We're patching you up. We're almost finished."

He was more than happy to lie perfectly still. Damn! What were they doing to his head? Didn't they believe in anesthetics?

"Four stitches," said a new voice, male. "That's nothing for a Saturday-night emergency. The nurse is going to get you bandaged, then we'll be moving you up to a room for overnight observation. We've called Dr. Kale. He's on his way."

Dr. Kale?

Tim became increasingly aware of the unique hospital smells and noises as the nurse dabbed and blotted, snipped and taped. His head throbbed. "Aspirin?" he asked, or tried to.

"Dr. Kale will take care of that," the nurse said. "He'll want to check you out first."

He tried opening his eyes to a squint until they adjusted to the light, then opened them the rest of the way. Machines. Rolling trays. Metal counters with canisters of swabs and cartons of gauze and sealed packets of disinfectant pads. God, he hated hospitals. He'd had his fill of them after the rafting disaster.

"How?" he said.

"You came in in an ambulance after a close encounter with an immovable object," the nurse informed him.

Tim tried to concentrate. At the hotel? No. Couldn't be. He'd had lunch with Tom, and then he'd gone to the beach until—

"What time is it?" he asked.

The nurse, a pleasant-looking woman in her forties, consulted her watch. "Just after nine."

"I missed the shuttle." He wiped his face with his hand. It was shaky. *After nine?* "I must have missed my flight, too. Wait a minute—" He tried to concentrate. Everything was fuzzy. "Did the doctor say it was Saturday?"

"It has been all day."

"Have I been unconscious?" *Even so, they wouldn't wait two days to stitch up a wound.*

"You'd better talk to Dr. Kale about that," she said.

"Who's Dr. Kale?"

"Your neurologist." She nodded toward the wide aisle separating the rows of treatment rooms, where an orderly was approaching with a gurney. "Looks like your limo is here. The floor nurses will get you settled into your room, and Dr. Kale will see you there."

In the waiting room in a different part of the hospital, Holly was pacing restlessly.

"If he's conscious, and he's in a room, why won't they let us see him?"

"You heard what they said. The neurologist wants to see him first," Josh said. "You know hospitals. They have their own way of doing things."

"What time is it?"

"Ten-twenty," Scalisi answered. He'd shown up about an hour after they arrived at the hospital, anxious to speak to Craig—Timothy—so he could close out the paperwork on his case.

"Seven minutes later than the last time you asked," Josh said. "Would you sit down, please. You're getting on my nerves."

"I can't just sit still."

"We'll deal you in on the next hand."

"I don't play poker."

Josh rolled his eyes and gave Scalisi a look of male camaraderie. "Too bad we don't have a fourth. We could have a bridge party."

"We'd have to send out for some of those little finger sandwiches," Scalisi elaborated.

"And a pot of tea," Josh said, affecting a British accent and holding an imaginary cup with his pinkie extended.

Holly stopped pacing and crossed her arms. "You guys are funny as a toothache."

"Hey, this is no picnic for any of us," Josh said. "It's Saturday night. I have a certain reputation to live up to."

"You said it," Scalisi agreed. "Marci had a baby-sitter lined up. We were supposed to go to a movie. I'll never hear the end of it."

"You don't have to stay on my account," Holly said.

"I drove you here, remember?" Josh said. "I can't leave you stranded."

"And I have a thousand loose ends to tie up with this case. Frankly, I'll be damned glad to get it off my desk."

"I'd kill for a beer," Josh said.

"You and me both," Scalisi said, shuffling the cards. "Are you sure you don't want us to deal you in, Holly?"

Another half hour passed before a distinguished-looking man in khaki jeans and a doctor's smock entered the room and looked around. "Officer Scalisi," he said as Scalisi rose to greet him. "It's good to see you again."

The doctor's name was Kale. Scalisi introduced Holly and Josh, explaining that Holly was a special friend of the patient's.

"I'm glad he has friends here," Dr. Kale said, pumping their hands enthusiastically. "I don't know how this case has been from your perspective, Officer Scalisi, but from my point of view, it's one of the most interesting I've encountered in eighteen years of specialty medical practice."

He paused to collect his thoughts, adopting a crisp, professional manner. "There's something I think you should know about your friend's condition."

Holly looked at him in alarm. "He's not—"

"Physically, he's fine. The bump on the head was superficial, little more than a nasty scratch. May I ask—were you with him when he was injured?"

"Yes. We were at my apartment," Holly replied.

"Do you mind telling me how it happened?" He listened with rapt attention as Josh and Holly gave a detailed account of the accident.

"So he was confronted with the information about his identity prior to the fall, and he showed indications of remembering his past?"

"Yes," Holly said. "The name seemed to bring everything back."

"He remembered the name of the grant he'd received," Josh volunteered.

Dr. Kale's mouth hardened into a straight line as he mulled over the information he'd just been told. At last, he said, "This is quite an interesting and complex case."

"What was it that you wanted to tell us?" Holly asked. "About Craig—Mr. Sotherland's—situation?"

"Your friend seems to have fully recovered his memory prior to the accident." He took a breath. "Or perhaps I should say, prior to the original accident."

"The original—do you mean when he was hit by the car?" Holly asked.

"Exactly," Dr. Kale said with a nod of emphasis. "Unfortunately, he seems to have lost the intervening interval between the two mishaps."

"He doesn't remember... *anything*?"

"He identified himself to me as Timothy Sotherland. He was aware he was in a hospital, but confused as to how he got here. He asked if I was Dr. Kale because the nursing staff told him to expect me. And when

I asked him if the name Craig Ford was familiar to him, he drew a total blank."

A total blank. The words sent a cold chill down Holly's spine. If he didn't remember the name he'd used as his own, he wasn't likely to remember hers.

"We'll work it out. No matter what happens, we'll work it out." But what if he didn't remember that there was anything he wanted to work out?

"He's unaware that he's lost a significant amount of time. He's concerned about having missed a seven-o'clock flight to London."

"He was supposed to catch that flight the day he was hit by the car," Josh said.

"I thought that might be the case," Dr. Kale said. "He's got to be told about the lapse. He's already complaining about the television in his room not working. If he catches on that we're deliberately keeping it off, he's going to be alarmed. I'd like to tell him before he has a chance to become too agitated."

"His head—is he strong enough?" Holly asked, concerned.

"I believe so." Dr. Kale looked at each of them. "I'd like you all to accompany me into his room. From what you've told me, he remembered his true identity when confronted with his name. It's possible that seeing someone familiar will jog his memory of the amnesiac period. If that happens, I'd like for him to be among friends. If not, he may have questions. Try to answer them calmly."

Numb, Holly walked with the others into the room. Craig—Timothy—was lying in the bed. A white bandage covered the gash behind and slightly below his ear.

It took every ounce of restraint she could muster not to rush to the bed and throw her arms around him.

He acknowledged their entrance with a friendly nod, but Dr. Kale was the only one to whom he spoke. Everyone else he regarded with benign curiosity, the way he would any stranger who'd wandered in.

"I've brought you some visitors," Dr. Kale said. "This is Holly Bennett—"

Holly held her breath as his gaze took in her face and lingered one or two seconds. His eyes registered male interest but not the slightest sign of recognition. "You can bring me visitors this pretty anytime," Craig said.

Timothy! Holly reminded herself. Timothy. *There was no Craig.* The name was different now, but the sexy, charming, slightly mischievous smile was so familiar and dear that it made her eyes burn with tears she could not shed. She felt as though someone had plunged a knife into her heart. How could he look straight at her and not know her, when mere hours earlier he had held her in his arms and told her that he loved her?

"And these are Officers Mick Scalisi and Josh Newmark. They may want to ask you a few questions."

"Officers?"

"Cocoa Police Department," Scalisi said.

"Police?" The hair on Tim's neck prickled. His instincts had been telling him something was askew ever since he woke up with this infernal headache. "Am I in some kind of trouble?"

"Not in the least," Officer Scalisi answered.

He was polite, but he didn't sound particularly reassuring. He sounded like a cop. And Tim's head hurt too badly to play cop games. "Then what's going on?"

"Please try to relax," Dr. Kale said.

Tim looked at the woman with them. The one with the big green eyes and face sweet enough to make a man's mouth water. "Are you a cop, too?"

She swallowed nervously. "I'm a librarian."

A librarian? She didn't look like any librarian he'd ever seen. "If this is about an overdue library book, there's got to be some mistake. I'm from Ohio."

Not a smile. Not even a twitch of amusement. Tim tensed involuntarily, which made his head throb even more. "What's wrong? My family?"

"Your family's fine," Scalisi said. "I talked to your sister earlier this evening. Everyone in Ohio is fine."

Tim wasn't buying it, not for a minute. "Look, my head may be hurting, but my brain still works. If everything's fine, why are cops talking to my sister?"

"Try to remain calm," Dr. Kale said.

"Did someone hit me over the head? Is that it? Have I been lying in an alley somewhere for two days?"

"What is the last thing you remember before waking up in the emergency room?" Dr. Kale asked.

"I've been trying to think back, reconstruct the day," Tim said. "I had lunch with Tom—"

"Tom who?" Scalisi asked.

"Tom Mitchell. He was my best friend in high school. He's stationed at Patrick Air Force Base. He's been after me for ages to fly down to Florida for a visit, so I routed my trip through Orlando. He picked me up there and brought me to Cocoa. We spent a couple of days doing the beach scene. After lunch on Thursday, he left for Patrick. I had a couple of hours before I had to catch the shuttle to the airport, so I decided to hang out at the beach a while. That's the last—"

He wiped his face with his hand. Damn, his head hurt. "Weren't you going to get me some aspirin or something?"

"Acetaminophen," Dr. Kale said. "It's ordered. The nurse should be bringing it anytime."

"Do you remember being at the beach?" Scalisi asked.

Tim closed his eyes and concentrated, then opened them. "Yeah. Yeah. We had lunch at that place out on the pier, and I stuck around there and then—"

It came back to him in a rush. "My wallet! Some guy jogging down the beach grabbed my wallet. I . . . ran after him." He looked at the cop who did all the talking. Scalisi. "It was him, wasn't it? I chased him up a side street. He ambushed me, didn't he? That's why you called my sister."

That explained it. He'd been notifying next of kin. But why his sister? Her last name was different. Wouldn't they have found his parents more easily?

"That's not exactly what happened," Scalisi said.

"Then what?"

It was the doctor who spoke this time. "You were brought in after being hit by a car."

"A car?"

"According to the driver, you ran right out in front of him," Scalisi said. "We've been trying to figure out why."

"I must have been chasing the guy, not paying attention—"

"That was one of our theories," Scalisi said. "Since you didn't have identification on you."

"No ID?" Tim said. He hoped that nurse showed up with the pain pills soon. "Oh. Of course. He had my wallet. Then how did you locate my sister?"

"Actually," Scalisi said, with a cautious exhalation, "your sister found us."

"I must have been hit on the head harder than I thought," Tim said. "None of this is making any sense. How would my sister—"

"She was checking your mail," Scalisi said. "Your wallet was returned by a Good Samaritan who found it in a trash can, cleaned out except for a video-store membership card with your name and address on it."

"How—did they send it by overnight mail? But—"

"You were brought in after the traffic accident as a John Doe," Dr. Kale said. "That was—"

Tim's guts curled with apprehension. What were they trying to tell him?

"—*some time ago*," the doctor completed.

"Some time?" Tim repeated. "As in . . . how much time?"

"Months."

Tim shook his head, denying the possibility. "Are you trying to tell me I've been . . . unconscious or something? That's impossible." They didn't send unconscious patients to the emergency room. And they didn't wait several months to sew them up. "But my head . . . they just sewed it up."

"This was a different injury," Dr. Kale said. "This time, you fell and bumped your head."

"A different . . . but—" Tim swallowed the lump of fear in his throat. "You're scaring me. How—"

"Can you tell me the date of the last day you remember?"

"Easy. It's the day I was going to leave for Europe."
He told them the date.

"That was the night you were brought in following
the automobile accident."

"But—you said it had been months."

"They brought you in as a John Doe," Dr. Kale reported. "You were relatively lucky. The car had slowed.
You had some nasty lacerations and a few broken ribs,
but the most serious injury was a concussion. You were
unconscious for thirty hours. When you regained consciousness, you showed no signs of the brain damage
we had feared, but you suffered an acute retrograde
amnesia."

"Amnesia? I couldn't remember anything?"

"Certainly not your name or any of your personal
history."

"I didn't know my own name?" Tim asked. It was too
fantastic to be believed.

"I was assigned to your case," Scalisi said. "We
monitored missing persons reports and put your picture out over the wire services. You were a tourist in
good physical health. Unfortunately, that was all we
had to go on."

"What—my family?"

"You were supposed to be in Europe," Scalisi said.
"At first, everyone was irritated that you didn't write,
but apparently you don't hang around post offices under the best of circumstances. Anyway, your sister assumed your parents were getting mail, and your parents
were up at their summer place in Wisconsin and assumed that they were getting mail at their house. When
they finally figured out no one had heard from you,

your sister remembered an odd call she'd gotten from an old high-school friend of hers. He asked if she knew how to get in touch with you, and gave her some story about a track team get-together. He was a cop in some little berg outside Chicago."

"Randy Holloway," Tim said. "He ran the four-hundred meter."

"Turns out he saw the picture of you and thought it looked like you, but he didn't tell her why he'd called, because she told him all about the award you'd won and your trip to Europe. He assumed our John Doe was just someone who looked like you. She got concerned and went through your mail and found the wallet and called the local cops, who put out a missing persons and gave us a call. As soon as we confirmed the identification, Officer Newmark went out to tell you the news."

"Your name triggered a return of your memory, you fainted and knocked your head on a table on the way to the floor," the doctor said.

Tim still couldn't believe it. Architects from Ohio didn't get hit by cars while chasing pickpockets in Florida and wake up with amnesia! "What—" He was almost afraid to ask. "What's today's date?"

The doctor told him.

Tim chortled at the irony. "Tomorrow's my birthday."

Something—he would have said it was a gasp, but he wasn't sure—drew his eyes to the librarian. The cop—the one who didn't say much—had his arm around her, which probably explained her presence. She looked—he was too upset himself to be particularly analytical—but she appeared unsettled about something. Her voice even sounded a bit strained as she asked, "How old will you be?"

Concentrating on the math made his head hurt. "Twenty-nine."

She paled, as if the answer somehow disturbed her. But Tim had too many problems of his own to give her reaction much thought. "If I haven't been unconscious, and I don't remember anything since the day I was supposed to fly to London, what...what was I *doing* for over three months?"

"You were assigned a social worker," Dr. Kale said. "You chose a name, and she helped get you situated in a furnished apartment. You've been working at the library."

Instinctively, he turned his attention to the librarian.

"Yes," the doctor said. "I believe you worked with Miss Bennett."

"I worked at a library?"

"You were a shelving assistant," Miss Bennett interjected helpfully.

"A shelving assistant? I shelved books all day?"

"You had no credentials," Dr. Kale said. "No social security number, for that matter."

It was all too much to comprehend. "This isn't a cruel practical joke by any chance, is it?" Tim asked, knowing it wasn't and wishing it could be.

Their faces confirmed his worst nightmare.

"I...I think I need some fresh air." The librarian. Speaking to the cop who still had his arm around her shoulders. "The hospital odors, I guess."

She forced an apologetic smile, and despite everything that was going on, Tim found the energy to feel a stab of envy for the cop comforting her.

"I'm glad the bump on the head wasn't too serious," she said. Then she hesitated oddly, as though choking on the words. Finally, she added, "Timothy."

11

"I SHOULD HAVE STAYED," Holly said. They were in Josh's car, on the way home from the hospital.

"You were pale as a ghost. I was ready to get you out of there even if you hadn't said anything," Josh said.

Holly rested her forehead against the side window. "You know what's ironic? I hadn't even thought about tomorrow being Craig's birthday." Her breath drew a hazy circle on the cool glass as she exhaled a weary sigh. How could she have forgotten Craig's birthday? "Not just the same date, but the same year."

"I know what you're thinking, Holly, but it's just another coincidence."

"I know. It's...it was all coincidence. All of it. But—" *The very same day of the very same year.*

"You're fogging the glass," Josh said.

"Sorry." She shifted away from the window.

Minutes passed before she spoke again. "I should have stayed."

"It's after midnight and you've had a rough night. One person collapsing is enough."

"He might have had questions."

"Scalisi and the doc can answer the questions he has right now. He's just trying to absorb the fact that he's lost some time. You can fill him in on the details later."

They had reached the apartment complex. Josh, gallantly, walked her to her door and offered to come in. Holly shook her head. "I could use some time alone."

Josh shrugged, kissed her cheek and left.

Holly had forgotten about the blood. The dark stain greeted her as she entered the apartment. For a few seconds, she stared at it with morbid fascination, wishing she had accepted Josh's offer to come in and keep her company. Then, suddenly, that ugly patch of drying blood became a symbol of every bad thing that had ever happened to her. Craig's death. Timothy Sotherland's betrayal—

Oh, yes. It was a betrayal, his failure to recognize her. Although she knew he had not chosen to forget her, she was not ready to forgive that lack of recognition. She was still too stunned, too wounded, too fragile from his rejection to be fair or forgiving. She would have been more tolerant, although no less hurt, if he had discovered that he had a wife. But to look at her as though he'd never seen her before, as though she were just any woman who'd chanced into his room—

It was crushing.

How many times had he assured her that if he'd had a wife, he would remember? How many times had he told her he could never forget her, or the love he felt for her? How many times had he said they would work it out, no matter what they found out?

Why did you just forget me, Timothy? Why couldn't you have been a wanted felon or something else just as simple.

With clenched-jaw determination, she attacked the stain with a large sponge, a can of carpet cleaner and a bucket of water. A quarter of an hour later, the spot was lighter, but still vivid against the pale gray carpet, and the water in the bucket was a hideous scarlet. Holly stared at the sponge, also dyed rusty red. Her shoulders slumped forward and she bowed her head, too weary to hold it upright. The thought that the blood in the sponge, in the bucket, in the carpet might be all that remained of . . . *Timothy* in her life flitted through her mind, but she dismissed it as the sick notion that it was. There was nothing left of him but her memories—the same memories his mind had misplaced.

As she knelt next to that accursed stain, holding the sullied sponge, the fear and disappointment of the day culminated in sobs that tore from her chest to clog her throat and wrack her shoulders. She cried until her throat was raw, her nose was red and every muscle in her body was sore and aching.

Finally, exhausted, she tossed the sponge in the trash and flushed the bloodied water down the toilet. Then she showered, put on her oldest, softest, rattiest sleep shirt and settled on the couch to watch Pepe Le Pew and eat part of the pizza that had arrived along with the paramedics hours earlier.

TIM STOOD in the center of the library, mystified and slightly disoriented as he surveyed the room. To one side, chrome and fake leather furniture provided a place to relax with a book, a newspaper or magazine and in front of him, book-laden shelves stood in straight lines like ranks of soldiers on a parade field.

It was like every library he'd ever seen, but there was absolutely nothing familiar about it. Could he really have worked here, spending hours—entire days— pushing carts of books between those shelves? Incredible, but true. He had the word of a neurologist, two cops and the owner of the Victorian house he'd been living in. Why would any of them lie?

Neither of the two woman running bar codes over electronic sensors at the checkout desk was the one who'd been in his hospital room. He'd been hoping to see her again, especially since Scalisi had told him she and the other cop who'd been in the room that night were just friends—which left him with a few questions. Like why she happened to be at the hospital. And why he was at her house when he fell and cracked his head.

One of the women spied him, flashed him a friendly smile and waved. As soon as she finished with the stack of books she was processing, she left the desk and walked over to him. "Hello."

"Hello," Tim replied, feeling at a distinct disadvantage, since she obviously knew him.

"It's good to see you," she said, then suddenly tried to cover self-consciousness with a nervous smile. "I guess we're supposed to call you Timothy now."

"Tim will do."

She held out her hand. "I'm Sarah. We . . . worked together . . . you know—"

"When I had amnesia," he said.

She nodded her head furiously, then said, "Holly told us about . . . everything."

Holly! The woman at the hospital.

"How's your head?"

"It's healing nicely, thank you."

Sarah chewed on her bottom lip thoughtfully, then asked, "Does anything . . . look familiar?"

"I wish it did."

An awkward silence followed. Finally, Tim said, "Would you do me a favor and tell everyone thank-you for the get-well basket?"

"Basket?"

"At the hospital. The card was signed 'The Library Staff.'"

"Oh. The basket Holly put together."

Holly again.

"You . . . uh, probably want to tell her thank-you. Personally, I mean."

She seemed to take it as a foregone conclusion that he would want to talk to Holly, which he found interesting. Scalisi's attitude regarding Holly had been equally intriguing. And with every assumption by the people who knew him as Craig Ford that he had a particular interest in Miss Holly Bennett, Tim's lists of reasons for wanting to talk to her grew longer. "Maybe I should."

"She's in the children's area. It's Story Hour, you know. Oh, you probably *don't* know. We have Story Hour on Thursday afternoons. They should be about half done."

After a moment, she prompted, "The, uh, children's area is down the center aisle, past those shelves and to the left, if you want to wait for her."

Tim did not miss the persistence in the librarian's voice or the anxiety in her attitude; he'd been the target of matchmakers often enough to recognize it for what it was. "Thanks," he said. "I'll do that."

From their brief encounter in his hospital room, Tim had a vague impression of Holly Bennett as pretty. When he reached the children's area and saw her seated in a chair surrounded by two dozen children, he decided that his head must have been hurting worse than he'd realized that night. Holly Bennett wasn't just pretty; she was just...plain...delicious. She not only had the face of an angel, she had a voice like honey and a smile like sunshine.

She was reading aloud about an English country goose with no sense of direction. The goose was trying to fly to her cousin's London house for tea and kept landing everywhere except in London, encountering an Irish setter in Ireland, a Scottish terrier in Scotland and a dachshund in Germany along the way. The children laughed rowdily as Holly read the part of the flustered goose with an English accent and breathed personality into each of the dogs she met on her pilgrimage. Her accents were far from perfect, but they were, without exception, adorable, and the children were charmed— along with Tim.

His suspicions that he and Holly had been more than cordial co-workers bore thorough investigation, he decided. He was stuck for at least a week while the travel agency tried to make sense of his botched travel arrangements. It might be nice to have some pleasant companionship while he waited.

The wayward goose ran into a French poodle named Charmaine and Holly's accent hit the tickle bone of a little boy in the audience. The child giggled aloud. "She sounds like Pepe Le Pew!"

"Yeah!" several of the children agreed. "Pepe Le Pew!"

If Tim hadn't been watching her so intently, he might have missed the way Holly suddenly tensed. He might not have caught the stricken expression that flitted over her face for just an instant before she put on a false smile that didn't reach her eyes. Up to that point, her attention had been directed either at the book she was reading or the children hanging on her every word, but now she looked up, over their heads.

Her face registered surprise as she spied Tim, and for several seconds, she seemed to lose her focus entirely, staring at him blankly. Then one of the children, the same boy who'd laughed about Pepe Le Pew, followed her gaze to Tim and announced, "It's the Big Bad Wolf!"

Giggles and titters followed, and Tim found himself the center of attention amid a flurry of comments about the Big Bad Wolf. What in the world were they talking about?

Finally, Holly snapped to attention to rescue him by distracting the children. "All right, guys. Settle down. Who remembers where Cicely Goose is and who she's talking to?"

They called out answers, and she resumed the story. "And what do you think Cecily Goose said when the poodle told her she was in France?"

Mimicking her English accent, the children answered in unison, "Oh, my! I daresay I've taken a wrong turn!"

Eventually, Cicely Goose found her way to London to have tea and biscuits with her city cousin, and the children applauded. But scarcely had the applause began to fade, when the precocious little boy who'd first spied Tim asked, "Will you read about the Three Little Pigs and the Big Bad Wolf again?"

The suggestion was met with much enthusiasm by everyone except Holly, who said, "We have another story to read this week."

"Please?"

Once again, Tim found himself the center of their attention as the boy was joined by a chorus of supporters, all of them talking about the Big Bad Wolf.

"Sounds like an encore performance is in order," Sarah said, walking up beside him.

"Encore?" Tim asked.

"You were quite a hit two weeks ago. They're not used to men at Story Hour."

Holly appeared acutely uncomfortable as she told the children, "I don't think Mr. Sotherland feels up to acting today."

The youngsters turned to him en masse, their eyes large with entreaty.

"Go for it!" Sarah said under her breath.

"Why not?" Tim said. Maybe he could make some strides toward renewing his acquaintanceship with Holly.

Holly looked anything but thrilled at his sudden capitulation, but before she could protest, Sarah jumped in and volunteered, "I'll get the book and the props."

Tim couldn't believe the props she brought back. He wouldn't have been so quick to agree to participate in the reading if he'd known he'd wind up wearing a headband with huge fake-fur ears. And as if the ears weren't bad enough, there was a tail. Long and fluffy, it dangled from a belt to well below his knees. He'd never felt as ridiculous in his life, although he supposed he'd have felt even more ridiculous if he'd been forced into wearing the ears, snout and springy pig's tail that Holly donned. No wonder she hadn't looked happy about the turn of events.

Sarah thrust an open book in his hand. "Here."

Holly began reading from a copy of the same book. What was expected of him became obvious when she reached a point in the narrative where the wolf spoke and she stopped abruptly and looked at him.

Feeling foolish, he read woodenly, "'Open the door and let me in!'" A brief passage of narrative led to his next line, "'I swear by the hair on my chinny-chin-chin—'"

The instant "chinny-chin-chin" rolled off his tongue, the children squealed with delight, and as the story progressed, Tim found himself playing to their enthusiasm, growing more and more boisterous with his lines.

Conversely, Holly seemed to grow more subdued, her voice becoming shriller and tighter as she read. And though she avoided looking at him, on those rare instances where their gazes connected, he saw the conflicting emotions in the depths of her eyes. And from the tension in her body, he got a clear impression that she was on the brink of running away from him as fast as she could, leaving the library, the children and the story behind.

Her attitude perplexed him. No fairy tale could disturb her so much. So it had to be him. His presence. But why? A hazy memory of her standing in his hospital room played through his mind. He'd thought she was with the cop because the man had his arm around her. But now he recalled thinking that she seemed upset about something. Scalisi had said she and the cop were just friends. If the cop had been comforting her—

The sound of someone clearing her throat shook him out of deep thought. "And the Big Bad Wolf *said*," she said pointedly, obviously not for the first time.

"'Open the door and let me in!'" he read, as anxious now as she clearly was to get to the end of the story—and to the bottom of what bothered Holly Bennett so much about being within ten feet of him.

After taking a leap into a cauldron of boiling water and howling appropriately, he took his bows as the audience, partly at Holly's urging, clapped their appreciation for his participation. Then, ears and tail in hand, he waited on the sidelines while Holly reminded the children that there was a Story Hour every Thursday afternoon. He noticed that she told most of the children goodbye individually as each left with a parent or sibling who'd come to collect them.

A tug on his arm drew his attention to the little boy who'd first noticed him. He'd been so involved in watching Holly that he hadn't seen the child approach.

"I'm sorry you got cooked in boiling water again," the boy said.

Tim grinned. The kid was about the age of his sister's son, to whom Tim had exclusive rights as favorite uncle. Winking, he tousled the boy's hair. "Maybe next time they'll let me be one of the pigs."

When the only children remaining in the area were sifting through picture books, Holly looked at Tim and squared her shoulders. He wanted to ask her right then why she seemed to dread any encounter with him so much, but that discussion was going to have to wait until they were in a less public setting.

"Thank you for being a good sport," she said. "I know the kids put you on the spot. They didn't realize—" Her eyes met his only briefly before she reached up to take off the pig's ears and snout, using the action to turn her head.

"How could they?" Tim asked. *And why can't you face me?*

He waited for her to speak next.

"How's your head?" she asked finally.

"The stitches itch."

She took a breath and exhaled wearily. "I didn't expect to see you here."

"I thought I'd take a look around."

"You still don't—" *She sounded too anxious, too interested to be a casual acquaintance.*

"No," he said. "Not a thing. I thought maybe something would look familiar, but . . ." He finished with a shrug.

"Well, at least you remember—" she hesitated, drew in a breath, as if fortifying herself "—everything else now."

"Yes. The only thing is, I don't even remember forgetting."

"Well, thanks again for being a good sport." She was dismissing him.

But Tim wasn't ready to be dismissed. "I came to— is there somewhere we could talk? Someplace a little less . . . a little more . . . private?"

"You could go into the break room," Sarah said. She must have been hovering, eavesdropping.

"I'm kind of busy," Holly said. She was a lousy liar. "Things are always chaotic after Story Hour."

"I'll stay in the area," Sarah volunteered. She stayed any further argument by flapping her hands at Holly, shooing her away. "Go on. The front desk has been slow. They'll never miss me."

Holly's reluctance was obvious, but she relented with a small shrug of her shoulders and led the way. The break room was furnished with a six-foot-long folding table, a few chairs and a kitchenette with a small refrigerator and sink. An eclectic assortment of mugs surrounded a coffeemaker on the diminutive work cabinet.

"Would you like coffee?" Holly offered. "Or a soft drink?"

"Thanks, anyway. I just want to talk."

"Talk?" she asked hoarsely, and Tim thought that he'd never seen a woman more uncomfortable. She hadn't actually looked at him since they'd entered the room.

"First, I wanted to thank you."

"Thank me?"

She was so taut, he thought that if he touched her she'd leap sky high. "For the gift basket."

"That was from everybody."

"Sarah said you put it together. It was a thoughtful thing to do."

"We were all concerned."

They may as well be reading a script of polite phrases, he decided. "German wine is my favorite," he said, determined to stray from the clichés.

"I looked for a label with *mit pradikat*."

"A fellow connoisseur."

"Not really. I just . . . knew you liked it."

How? The question was there, on the tip of his tongue, but he couldn't ask it. It would be too abrupt.

"Scalisi said I was at your house when I fell."

She nodded, but didn't elaborate. She was hugging herself, as though awaiting life-and-death news.

"He said we were friends."

The head bobbed again. A long silence ensued. Finally, Tim said, "What was I doing at your house, Holly?"

"Apartment," she said. "I live in an apartment."

"The question stands. What was I doing there?"

"We were—" The words came out painfully slow. "Watching a movie on television."

"We were more than friends, weren't we?"

"Yes," she said, scarcely above a whisper.

"Were we . . . intimate?"

At first, he wasn't sure she was going to answer. She stood eerily still, avoiding his gaze, until a sigh shuddered through her. Finally, for the first time since they'd entered the room, she looked at him. He read the answer to his question in her eyes before the word *yes* hissed from her throat.

"I don't know what to say to you," he told her.

"You don't have to say anything. When we were together, I knew that everything was . . . crazy."

In his entire life, he'd never seen anyone more vulnerable.

"There are no etiquette books to cover this situation," he said. He ached to wrap his arms around her and comfort her, but he dared not, unless she reached out for him.

She didn't. Nor did she speak.

Unable to resist touching her, Tim cradled her face in his hands, noting the softness of her skin beneath his fingers. She stared up at him as if transfixed by his gaze, her eyes filled with sadness. "I'm sorry, Holly. I wouldn't—"

Covering his left hand with hers, she guided it from her face. "You have nothing to apologize for. I knew—" She turned her head away. "At least now you have your life back—your name, your family, your career."

Taking her hint, Tim allowed his right hand to drop to his side. "Something tells me I'm going to spend the rest of my life regretting not being able to remember being with you."

Tension weighted the ensuing silence until, finally, Holly asked, "So—are you going home soon?"

"I'm going to go ahead with the European tour first."

"That's . . . nice."

"I've always wanted to go and take in the architecture. The timing's right, now." He hesitated, then decided to take a chance. "The travel agency is working on rescheduling everything. It's probably going to take another week. Would you—could we—go out for dinner or something?"

"I don't think so."

There was finality in her voice, so he didn't pursue the issue. Tim's mind teemed with questions, but he found himself at a loss for words. Suddenly, he felt profound sadness, as though he'd lost something very dear. "Well—"

"I should get back to work," she said.

He nodded. "I'll walk you back."

"No!" she said quickly. "You go on. I . . . have some things I need to get out of the storage room."

Tim nodded. He didn't want to leave, but it seemed his only alternative.

"Mr. Sotherland?" Her voice stopped him just as he reached the door.

Tim stopped and turned to her expectantly.

"You have a scar on your chest," she said. "Do you mind if I ask how you got it?"

Tim chuckled. "Not at all. I had a nasty encounter with a tree limb while white-water rafting."

"It looks serious."

"It was—or could have been. All things considered, I was pretty lucky. A fraction of an inch in either direction and I'd have been meeting my Maker that day."

"Do you remember when the accident happened? The date?"

"I ought to. I filled out enough insurance papers." He told her the date.

She paled. "That would have been...just over a year ago."

"I suppose it would," he said. "It doesn't seem that long." He shrugged. "Time flies when you're having fun, huh?"

She tried to smile as she acknowledged his attempt at humor with a nod.

12

"A FRACTION OF AN INCH in either direction, and he'd have been dead," Holly said. "Josh, do you remember the doctor talking about the bullet that hit Craig? He said if it had just been a fraction of an inch over in either direction, Craig would be alive."

Josh stopped pacing the floor long enough to run his hands through his hair. "It's just another screwy coincidence."

"How many coincidences do you have to have before they're not coincidences anymore?" Holly asked. "He was born the same day as Craig, and he almost died the day Craig died."

"The bullet was a fraction of an inch in the wrong direction and Craig died. The branch was a fraction of an inch in the right direction, and Timothy Sotherland survived. Timothy Sotherland was lucky. Craig wasn't." He sat down next to Holly and lifted her hands in his. "You know how Craig felt about the danger cops are in. If your number's up, it's up. If it's not, it's not. His number was up. Sotherland's number wasn't. If Craig was here, he'd tell you the same thing. You know he would."

Holly exhaled a sigh that left her shoulders drooping. Then she looked at Josh's face and tried to smile. "I think I just needed to hear you tell me that. I'm trying to look for some kind of reason where there isn't any."

Dropping her hands, Josh leaned back, slumping against the back of the couch. "I never thought it would work out this way."

"Join the club."

"For what it's worth, I was really hoping things would work out for you and the Amnesia Kid."

"You were? Mr. Jaded Suspicious Cop himself?"

"Someone had to look at things objectively, Holly. I was concerned about you. I was afraid he was conning you, and I didn't want to see you hurt."

Holly laughed bitterly. "The good news is, he wasn't conning me. The bad news is, once he got his memory back, he didn't even remember my name." A tear trailed down her cheek as she looked at Josh and asked, "How could he just . . . *forget* me?" She wiped the tear away with her palm and sniffed. "Damn! I thought I was all cried out."

"I may be a jaded old cop, but the shoulder's still absorbent," Josh said, holding out his arms in invitation.

Holly shook her head and sniffed determinedly. "No. I refuse to fall apart." She forced a smile. "But do me a favor, okay? Next time I decide to fall in love, remind me to find a nice, safe accountant from Orlando."

"What's wrong with a promising hotshot architect from Ohio?"

"The one who looked straight at me from his hospital bed and had no idea who I was?"

"Why don't you cut the guy a little slack, Holly? He can't help it if he has amnesia. Why don't you talk to him, tell him how things were?"

"I just can't do it that way," Holly said. "Not after—"

"You're just going to let him walk out of your life without even telling him how things were between the two of you?"

"He figured it out," she said, and then scowled. "Enough to know he'd been in my bed, anyway. He offered to take me to dinner. I think he was hoping for a quickie for the road."

"Are you sure that's what he wanted?"

She shrugged desolately. "He was suave about it, but it was on his mind."

"Holly! Of course it was on his mind. The chemistry between the two of you was explosive. Do you know what it would do to a man to look at a pretty woman and know he'd been with her?"

"I believed in him!" she said. "Even when it wasn't logical, I believed in him, because he said that he would know if he loved someone, even if he didn't remember names or faces. He said he'd feel it inside."

Her eyes searched Josh's face for understanding. "He said he loved me. If he loved me so much, why doesn't he *feel* it, the way he was so sure he'd *feel* if he'd had a wife?"

"He may yet."

"All he had to do was hear his name and he remembered his past. He looked me straight in the face and nothing clicked. *Nothing.*"

"It was months before he heard his name and regained his memory, Holly. And then he had another bump on the head. Who's to say he won't remember you and everything about you a few weeks from now?"

"He'll probably have a lover in every country in Europe by then."

"The guy has that much stamina?"

"If that's supposed to be wit, I'm not in the mood."

Josh shrugged. After a contemplative pause, he said, "You know what's really ironic? When I saw that missing persons report come in and found out that he was straight as an arrow, I did a lot of thinking about your saying I was jaded and suspicious."

"I was probably a little hard on you," Holly said.

"Probably?" he asked sarcastically.

"You surprised me. I was so caught up in Craig's situation that I wasn't expecting suspicion."

"You said I'd been a cop too long, and that this was Cocoa, Florida, not New York or Chicago."

Holly winced. "I *was* a bit harsh, wasn't I?"

"Actually, I probably ought to thank you."

"For being tacky?"

"For giving me something to think about. You were right. I have become jaded. And I am frustrated on a small-town force. I've been...I don't know...at loose ends ever since Craig was killed. I've been asking myself what it's all about. Your comments made me do a little soul-searching, and I've come to realize that I'll never be happy being a cop in Cocoa."

"You're not thinking of leaving the force?"

"In a manner of speaking, I am."

"I can't imagine you as anything but a cop."

"How about as an FBI agent?"

"FBI?"

"I've always wanted to get into the real meat of police work—crime-scene analysis. Where else would I get such great training and challenging cases?"

Josh in the FBI. It was perfect. "Have you done anything about this yet?"

"I talked to an agent yesterday, and I've requested all the applications. I'll probably have to finish up my degree—I left a couple of semesters before graduating—but my experience on the force and the career-enrichment courses I've taken should work in my favor."

Holly drew in a breath and released it abruptly. "I'm astounded. I . . . I think it's great, Josh. I hope it works out for you."

"If it does, you can come to the academy at Quantico when I graduate."

"I think Craig would be happy for you, too."

"Craig would have been right beside me," Josh said. He chortled bitterly. "Too bad I didn't think of it sooner."

"At least a couple of people are getting happy endings out of this mess."

"I am," he said. "Who else is?"

"Timothy Sotherland," she said tautly. "He's flying off to Europe for the grand tour of old-world architecture."

"You should go right over to that old Victorian house and tell him exactly how things were between you," Josh said. "What do you have to lose?"

"I would have told him if he'd asked," Holly said, and then stared into space. "Unfortunately, he didn't ask the right questions."

"ARE YOU GOING to be in town long?" the server asked.

The hope in the seemingly innocuous question was impossible to miss. She was an attractive girl, with sun-streaked hair that fell well below her shoulders and tanned legs long enough to tweak a man's imagination. And she was his for the asking.

But Tim wasn't asking. He'd spent the better part of the past several days on the beach watching long-legged women in bikinis with sun-streaked hair and he hadn't asked any of them. He attributed his reticence to the lingering effects of his injuries. Although physically, he was almost as good as new, the shock of everything he'd been through had left him in the throes of some type of lethargy of the spirit. He'd lost a piece of his life. He was not depressed, but his foundation had been rattled. The shake-up had left him more aware of the details of his life, and the idle time he found on his hands waiting on his stitches to come out so he could be on his merry way to England and other European destinations had given him a rare opportunity for reflection and evaluation.

He was lucky and he knew it. He'd been blessed with a loving family, an extraordinary talent and the education to refine and enhance it. He'd survived one nearly fatal accident and a second potentially fatal one. The award he'd just won cast a rosy hue on his future. His professional future was chock-full of promises; all he had to do was deliver performance for expectation. He was off to a grand tour of many of the finest architectural wonders of the world and he would come home to a commission that would enable him to combine skill and creativity into the realization of a vision.

If the plane didn't crash, he thought wryly. Two brushes with death made a man aware of such possibilities. Just as it made him look more closely at his life and his priorities. Having lost the months between his lunch with Tom Mitchell and his fall in Holly Bennett's

apartment, it seemed as if scarcely a week had passed
since he and Tom had cruised the same beach in search
of an easy conquest. They'd sat on beach chairs under
rented umbrellas and discussed body parts the way
they'd have discussed antilock brakes or rear spoilers
on cars in a showroom, rating breasts and legs and butts
without sparing a single thought to the fact that they
were looking no deeper than skin and muscle. They
were bachelors on the prowl, accountable to no one,
out for a good time, enjoying their freedom.

They'd talked to a few of the women, sharing soft
drinks from the cooler Tom had brought, but their
conversation had been as superficial as their appraisal
of the women's physical attributes. They'd exchanged
names and hometowns and job titles and discussed the
merits of particular brands of tanning lotions. The
women had been impressed by the fact that Tim was on
his way to Europe and that Tom was a pilot. They'd
asked about the scar on Tim's chest and the tattoo Tom
had gotten when he was dead drunk following his
graduation from the first phase of flight school. There
had been idle suggestions that they might meet on the
beach again, but no times had been set.

That night, when Tim and Tom—the Terrible T's as
they were called in high school—retired to their hotel
suite to pig out on pizza, reminisce about old times and
catch up on everything that had happened to each other
since they'd gone off to their respective colleges, they'd
laughed about how they'd both outgrown the "any girl,
anywhere, anytime, any way" mentality. Tom was
seeing a career air-force dentist he'd met at his previous
duty station and hoping she could get assigned to Patrick. And Tim had admitted that he was growing weary

of the chase and wouldn't mind finding a steady woman of his own.

Now, three months-that-seemed-like-a-week after that admission to his childhood buddy, he was giving much thought to his life. The rafting accident had been a "ha-ha" close call, but his second brush with death so soon afterward had impressed upon him how tenuous life really was. His number had not come up, but he had been made aware that anybody's number could come up at any time—even Timothy Sotherland's. He walked the beach communing with nature and thinking about what he'd have left behind if his number *had* come up. Or if it came up tomorrow.

The answers he discovered were less than satisfying. Life had been good to him and he was a good person, but if he had died when he'd encountered that tree limb or when he'd taken on a moving car, he'd have left behind a legacy of promise rather than one of achievement. Everything he had to be grateful for, he'd been handed on a silver platter: his family, his talent, his looks. Everything he'd achieved could be traced back to the family who'd nurtured him or the talent that came from his gene pool. He was on the threshold of a new phase in his life. The foundation was laid; it was time to build on that foundation. He was ready to make his contribution to the world, to leave a mark. If his number came up, he wanted to leave behind something positive to show he'd been there.

On Sunday, the beach had been packed with families. Tim had looked at couples and felt alone. He'd looked at children and wondered what it would be like to be a parent. He'd looked at grandparents and contemplated the continuity of generations. He'd looked at the occasional long-legged beach girl and thought of a librarian with a pretty face and green eyes as readable as any book.

Today, Monday, he left the pier restaurant and slogged through the soft sand, thinking about Europe. The travel agency had called to say they were expressing his new tickets. A visit to the doctor to get rid of his stitches and then he'd be catching the bird to the opposite shores of the ocean he was wading in.

Alone.

He'd never given any thought to that aspect of the trip. He had too much to see, too much to learn. The award had opened doors for him. He'd be meeting architects in almost every city on his itinerary. It had not occurred to him that he would be doing it all alone. Enchanted by the prospect of all that beauty, he had never considered that he might enjoy it more sharing it with someone. Not until he'd watched couples at the beach, holding hands, running together, laughing. Young couples walking with their children between them. Older couples walking with decades of shared lives linking them.

He left the beach and drove to the Victorian house. He still found it hard to believe he'd lived so long in a two-room suite with carved molding, rose-splashed wallpaper and a lumpy single bed. Encased by plastic shower curtains hung on a curved rod suspended from the ceiling, he showered in the claw-foot tub and then changed into fresh clothes.

He did not actually decide to go to the library. He just went, realizing as he walked into the hushed atmosphere that he was in search of answers that would not be found between the covers of the books shelved here.

He didn't see Holly in the children's area, but he lingered there, remembering the richness of her voice as she read to the children, the charming, if inept, accents she'd used to portray the English goose and the dogs from Ireland, Scotland, Germany and France.

"Tim. I thought I saw you come in."

It wasn't the voice Tim had been hearing in his mind. He turned. "Hello, Sarah."

"Holly doesn't come in on Mondays."

"I wasn't—" He grinned sheepishly. "Yes, I was."

"She'll be in tomorrow."

"I'll try to make it in tomorrow." He grinned again, and nodded. "I'll be back."

"Those are the flowers you sent," Sarah said, indicating a basket of cut flowers atop one of the waist-high shelves in the children's area. "They're still pretty. I gave them fresh water first thing this morning."

"The florist did a good job," Tim agreed. "Good." *They had been sent to Holly—why hadn't she taken them home with her?*

"You must be thoroughly confused," Sarah said. "I mean, it must be strange to come back here, and not be able to remember."

"Yes," he said. "Strange is a good word for it." As good as any, he supposed. And as inadequate. She obviously knew Holly well. He still wasn't sure what the questions were, but he wasn't going to pass up a chance to get answers. "Sarah, I know you're working, but do you get a break any time soon? Could we go somewhere for a cup of coffee?"

She gave him a long, hard look. "This is about Holly, right? I mean, she's a friend of mine."

Tim smiled. "And you're obviously a very good friend to her." He was so preoccupied with Holly, that it hadn't occurred to him that Sarah might think he was coming on to her. "Yes," he assured her. "This is about Holly."

Sarah glanced at her watch. "I could take a few minutes."

Images of Holly assailed him as they entered the break room. Holly's face. Holly's eyes. Holly, avoiding his gaze. Holly, hurt and trying to hide it. Holly, admitting they'd been lovers after she'd been introduced to him in his hospital room and he hadn't known who she was.

"How do you like your coffee?" Sarah asked.

"I don't want coffee," he said. "You go ahead." He waited for her to fill her mug at the coffeepot and carry it to the table, where she dropped into one of the plastic chairs. He sat down opposite her.

She took a sip of the steaming coffee, then set the mug on the table, leaving her hands wrapped around it. "You must have a million questions."

He shrugged. "If I just knew what they were."

"Holly?" she said with a sly grin.

Tim smiled. "Tell me about her."

"What's to tell?" Sarah said. "She was born to be a children's librarian. You saw her at Story Hour. She can get kids interested in books faster than anyone I've ever seen. She had you checking out *Make Way for Ducklings*."

"*Make Way* . . . the one about the mother duck crossing the street with all her ducklings? I read that in second grade. I saw the statue in Boston."

"She said you didn't remember reading it."

"I guess I didn't." He'd forgotten everything—his name, his history, the books he'd read, the people who'd meant so much to him. What a nightmare! It was probably a blessing he couldn't remember the experience. He was shaken enough over losing a few weeks.

"She's good with children," he said.

"Holly loves children. She was planning to have one right away."

"She what?" Tim asked with a trace of panic.

"Not with you," Sarah said, with a nervous laugh. "With Craig."

Tim paled.

"Not Craig Ford. With the other Craig." She exhaled in frustration. "I guess you don't know. How could you? Holly was engaged to a man named Craig. That's one of the reasons she didn't want to go out with you at first."

"*One* of the reasons?"

"You worked here," Sarah said with a shrug. "She was afraid it would get awkward."

"When I was here last week, I got the distinct impression that you were playing matchmaker."

Sarah watched him over the rim of her mug as she took another sip of coffee. "And you want to know why."

Tim nodded, and she put down the cup. "Holly is a very private person," she said. "She doesn't—I hate to resort to clichés—but she's not the type to kiss and tell. So I don't know everything about what went on between the two of you. But she was happy when you were together, and Holly deserves to be happy after—"

She hesitated.

"You might as well tell me," Tim prompted. "Did the Craig she was engaged to break her heart?"

"He was a cop. He was killed just weeks before the wedding."

"God." He hadn't been expecting that.

"Holly was devastated. Meryl—she's another one of the librarians—and I thought she'd never . . . and then you came to work here and it was obvious what was going on, so—" She smiled.

"What was going on," Tim thought aloud. "What was so obvious?"

Sarah rose unexpectedly. "I could try to explain, but it would be easier to show you." She left the room and returned a few minutes later carrying a videocassette. "I taped Story Hour the first time you were the wolf." She inserted the film into a videocassette recorder hooked up to a television set on a rolling cart. Handing Tim the remote control, she said, "It's ready to play. I've got to get back to work."

Tim pressed the play button after Sarah left the room. He stared at the images on the screen transfixed. Could that really be him wearing fur ears and exchanging sizzling looks with the angel-faced librarian?

Had the angel-faced librarian in a red plastic cape really looked at him that way?

"Oh, Grandma, what big eyes you have!" she read sweetly from the text.

"The better to look at you as though I could devour you!" his expression said.

He continued staring at the screen long after the images were replaced by snow. No wonder Holly had been uncomfortable when he'd been drafted into an encore performance as the wolf. The two people he'd seen on that tape had been totally involved with each other. And one of them had erased that involvement from his memory as easily as the images could be erased from the tape.

He rewound the tape and started it again, studying Holly's face this time, wondering how it was possible for any man to forget a woman's looking at him the way she looked at Craig Ford.

Craig Ford. Who was this man with his face, his body, his mannerisms?

The tape was still playing when a woman entered the break room. She greeted him familiarly on her way to the coffeemaker, where she poured coffee for herself before proceeding to the table. "That's a hoot, isn't it?"

Tim stopped the film. "It's . . . interesting."

"Sarah was going to add it to our video collection, but we weren't sure whether to put it under children's or start a new adults-only list."

"I'm sorry," Tim said. "I probably know—*knew*—you, but—"

"Of course! You don't have the faintest idea who I am. I'm Meryl. Front desk. And I guess I need to call you Timothy now, instead of Craig."

"Tim's good enough." He shook his head, perplexed. "I don't know where 'Craig' came from. The doctor said I chose the name, but I must have pulled it out of the air."

"In a way, you did," Meryl said. "Holly said you got it from a character on a soap opera. A hunky, playboy type."

"I watched soap operas?"

"In the hospital. You were a captive audience."

Tim muttered a very strong expletive then begged Meryl's pardon. "I don't usually use language like that, but this situation sucks."

"It's one humdinger of a situation," Meryl agreed dryly.

"I guess you know Holly, too."

"Around here, she and Sarah and I are known as the Three Stooges."

"So, did you really come in to drink coffee, or do you plan to lure me into a pot of boiling water?"

"It was time for my break," she said. "Not that I wouldn't gleefully boil you like a lobster if I thought you had deliberately set out to break her heart."

"I didn't." Tim drew in a breath and exhaled tiredly. "I'm sorry she's hurt. Maybe you'll tell her—"

"Sorry," Meryl said. "I never get involved in romantic intrigues. The messenger is the one who usually gets shot."

Tim released a sigh of utter defeat.

"Back at you, buddy," Meryl said. "The last thing anybody around here wanted was to see Holly hurt again." She frowned. "You know, none of us thought it would work out this way. When Holly told us about your amnesia, we were all afraid you'd get your memory back and remember that you were married."

Tim used the expletive again. "I hadn't even thought about that. But Holly—"

"Holly took a leap of faith. You told her that if you loved someone, there was no way you could forget that feeling, even if you didn't remember details. You said you didn't *feel* married or *think* like a married man. Holly swallowed it, hook, line and sinker."

Meryl paused to take a sip of coffee. "Holly still believes in people. She'll get over it, if she hasn't already."

"I'd like to—" *To what?* he wondered. *To fix everything? To undo what he couldn't even remember?*

"Talk to her," he said, not knowing where the words came from. "Can you tell me where she lives?"

"Nope!" Meryl said. "It's against library policy to give out addresses of employees."

Tim scowled in frustration.

"However, we do keep a current residential city telephone directory in reference, and if you looked up a person's address and asked for directions to a certain street, we'd probably be able to sketch a map."

Tim gave her a wry smile. "Where's reference?"

HOLLY PULLED ON her lace cover-up and tucked her wadded towel under her elbow. The late-afternoon swim had been refreshing. Now, if she could just get through the evening...

Following the walk, she turned from the side of her building to the front, then froze when she spied a man standing at her door. Waiting. She recognized him instantly. It was Craig Ford. Or the man who had been Craig Ford. *The man she was in love with. The man who'd forgotten her.*

She stepped back, out of sight, and waited for him to leave. Minutes seemed like hours before a peep around the corner revealed that he was finally leaving. His shoulders drooped dejectedly as he walked. If he were still Craig Ford, if they were still lovers, she would wrap her arms around him and whisper sweet sentiments in his ear. But he was a stranger. A stranger who looked so much like Craig Ford that her heart ached when she saw him.

When he was out of sight, she proceeded to her apartment.

"Holly?"

Her heart lodged in her throat at the sound of his voice.

He rounded the row of tropical shrubs in front of the building at a quick jog. "I thought I saw you. I had just about given up, but I saw you from my car."

"Who gave you my address?" she asked, phrasing the question like an accusation. He couldn't remember her name—how would he know where she lived?

"I looked it up in the phone book."

The lock yielded to a twist of her key. Holly turned the knob, but didn't push open the door. "What are you doing here?"

"May I come in?"

She might have remained strong if he had left it at that, but he didn't. Soft as dandelion fluff, he added, "Please?"

Please, she thought, squeezing her eyes shut as her fingers convulsed around the doorknob. Summoning her courage, she nodded and opened the door, letting him in.

No matter what he calls himself, no matter how bizarre the situation, you're always letting him in—when are you going to be strong enough to turn him away?

Inside, she suddenly found herself at a loss for words. Finally, self-consciously looking down at her lace-shielded swimsuit and bare legs, she said, "I need to rinse the chlorine out of my hair. It'll only take a few minutes."

"I'll wait," he said, smiling sweetly enough to break her heart all over again.

Holly dallied in the shower, taking longer than usual to lather her hair and standing under the flow of hot water long after the shower gel was rinsed from her skin. She did not want to face him. She did not want to thank him for the flowers he'd sent or field his questions or listen to him tell her once more how sorry he was that he could not remember the time they'd spent together. Most of all, she didn't want to face the possibility that he might suggest a cozy little dinner, which he doubtless would hope might lead to a cozy little romp in her bed.

Trembling, she turned off the water and pressed her forehead against the wall of the shower stall. *It was over and done with. Dead. Why couldn't he just . . . leave it alone? Leave her alone?*

Her thought process was paralyzed. She couldn't decide what clothes to put on, or whether to blow her hair dry or just slick it back. Eventually, she selected shorts and a blouse and dried her hair. Then, with her cheeks flushed from the heat of the dryer and her hair hanging loose around her face, she returned to the living room.

He stood when she entered the room, and she felt his gaze, warm and curious, on her as she walked. Too restless to sit, she stopped behind the armchair facing the one in which he'd been sitting and rested her hands on the back. He was still looking at her, studying her face.

Shaking his head as though dazed, he said, "I circled the block for almost two hours before I found the courage to stop."

She leaned against the chair, glad it was there to support her. "Why did you?" she asked stoically. "What do you want from me?"

He stepped forward until he just a few feet away from her. "I think I'm losing what's left of my mind."

"There must be someone you could talk to. A doctor, or social worker—" *Don't ask me to help you; I'm hurting too much. I've given you all I have to give. I'm falling apart just being this close to you.*

"I think I miss you," he said.

"You remember—"

He raised his hand in a halting gesture. "No. No. But listen. Please. I know it doesn't seem to make any sense." His hands balled into fists. "I don't...*remember*. Not meeting you. Not the details. But...something Meryl said—"

"You talked to Meryl? At the library?"

"Come over here," he said, leading her to the couch. "Sit down and try to follow me. I'm probably not explaining it well, but—"

He let his shoulders droop against the back of the couch and exhaled wearily. "I went to the beach," he said. He lifted his hands, palms up, gesturing for emphasis. "I went to the beach, and I felt...*alone*. I was looking at the couples and feeling like part of me was missing. I've never felt that way before. I didn't feel that way when I went to the beach the days before my accident."

"What does Meryl have to do with this?" Holly said, trying to follow.

"She said that when I had amnesia—the first time—that I told you I didn't believe I was married because I didn't feel married, and that I was sure if there had been someone I cared about that I would know it, even if I didn't remember." His chortle held a note of self-derision. "She seemed to think you were gullible to swallow it."

"Meryl's been around the block a few more times than I have."

"It makes sense," he asked, weighting each word with intensity. "I don't recall the details, but I...emotionally, I must be remembering the... unity. I felt like part of a couple and I missed the other half. I must have been missing you."

Afraid to believe, Holly said, "You're feeling disoriented. You're grasping at our relationship because you know about it."

"I saw the tape, Holly. The Story Hour video. The way we looked at each other—"

"But you still don't remember!" she said.

"I can't help that!" he said, plunging his hand into his hair again. "Don't you think I would, if I could?"

"I know you would," she whispered hoarsely. *But you don't!* She might be able to forgive him with her rational mind, but her irrational heart couldn't forget the betrayal.

"But we're the same people. Inside. In the places we feel affection and attraction. What I felt for you couldn't have just...dissolved."

She was staring down at her hands in her lap. He grabbed her upper arms. "Look at me. Listen to me." Slowly, she raised her head until her eyes locked with his. "Maybe there are different types of memories," he said. "Maybe some are like photographs full of detail, but others—others could be more like, I don't know, electrical impulses or waves, like television signals.

Maybe all I have left about us is invisible waves. That doesn't make *us* any less real to me inside."

He heaved a sigh that revealed his frustration. "I'm not a psychiatrist or a philosopher. I don't know all the theory. All I know is that when I look into your eyes, I see something calling to me. I see the same loneliness I feel now, a loneliness I didn't feel before."

Holly's heart lodged in her throat. *The same loneliness. Oh, God, he saw it too. Maybe—*

"What do you want?" she asked. "What are you saying?"

"I'm saying that I think there's something between us. Something too precious to lose. Something we should hold on to or, at least, explore."

Explore? In the bedroom, perhaps? She was afraid to let herself believe anything else. "What we had— when we were together—wasn't something we could explore in a few days."

"I want you to come with me," he said.

"Come with you?"

"To Europe."

"Europe?" *He was right. He had lost what was left of his mind.*

"I know it sounds crazy. And I know it's short notice."

"Short notice? Europe in . . . *days?* That's not short notice, it's—"

"It's . . . once-in-a-lifetime," he said. "The award I won came with a cash endowment, and I decided to take the trip of a lifetime. I'm going to soak in all the old-world architecture while I'm there, but I want to experience it all, especially—"

He paused for breath. "I could have been killed. For the second time in two years. Now I want to take it all in, every bit of it, everything I can. And I want to share it, all of it, and who better to share it with than a woman who looks at me the way you do?"

"H-how do I look at you?" she stammered.

"What's the line from that old movie? *The Sound of Music.* 'Nothing is more irresistible to a man than a woman who's in love with him.' When I look into your eyes, I see love, and something in me is answering it."

"I don't..." Her voice trailed off. What could she say? She couldn't deny that she loved him when her eyes were telling him the truth.

"Come with me, Holly," he said, taking her hands in his. "No strings. We could have separate rooms, and you'd be free to come home anytime you want. I'll let you hold the return ticket."

"But my job—"

"Take a leave of absence," he said. "Haven't you ever dreamed about just getting on a plane and taking off? Haven't you ever read books and thought you'd rather live it than read it? Let's do it together. Let's hop from country to country like that English goose and see if we can find our way back to what we had. What would we have to lose?"

Holly stared at him mutely, unable to think of a single thing they had to lose. Her mind was too busy counting up the things they might gain.

13

EVEN BEFORE she forced an eye open to search for the glow-in-the-dark dial of the travel clock, Holly was quite sure that it was not time for any alarm to be going off. A slight twist of her head brought the clock into her field of vision just as a male hand slapped the control. The irritating buzz ceased.

"W-w-w?" Holly stammered, which was her middle-of-the-night way of asking what time it was and why the alarm was going off. They'd rarely set an alarm clock on the entire trip.

"Up, sleepyhead," Tim said, chuckling. He'd turned out to be almost despicably cheerful first thing in the morning, in contrast to Holly, who required a few minutes to adjust to the idea that it was time to wake up.

"Why? What time—*five forty-five?* What are you doing getting me out of bed at five forty-five?"

"You'll see," he said, blatantly flaunting good cheer. "It's a surprise!"

Holly rolled over, pulling the pillow over her head. "Surprise me at nine."

Tim grabbed the pillow and tossed it to the foot of the bed. "It's now or never, sweetheart."

"Never!"

"If you don't get up, you'll spend the rest of your life wondering what you missed."

"Tyrant!" Holly muttered, pushing up on her arms. "Bully."

"If you don't quit calling me names, I'm going to wash your mouth out with soap," he teased. He was already up, pulling on a pair of jeans.

"You and whose army?" Holly said, dropping her feet to the floor.

Tim knelt next to her and picked up one of her slippers. "Here, Cinderella. See if this fits. We don't want your tootsies getting cold."

She cooperated while he put the shoes on her feet, and then put her arms into her chenille housecoat when he held it up for her. "I should probably brush my hair," she said.

Grinning, he mussed it. "You know I think it looks sexy when you first get out of bed."

"Well, I just hope that wherever we're going, we don't run into any small children. I'd probably scare them."

"There won't be any children," he said, grabbing her hand.

They were in a guest house outside of Bergenz, Austria. Their room was on the second floor. Tim escorted Holly up the uneven wooden steps to the third story and then on to the attic floor, where a tiny door opened onto an observation platform.

Tim stood behind Holly and wrapped his arms around her, folding them across her shoulders above her breasts. Stars glistened in the deep blue sky like diamonds strewn on velvet.

"The sky is the same color as your eyes," Holly said, resting her head against his chest.

"Not for long," he said, propping his chin on the top of her head. "This deck faces east." Already, a streak of white haloed the tops of distant mountains.

The streak widened with an arrogant lethargy until, finally, the faintest suggestion of a curve emerged over one crest, spilling light over the tree-covered mountains. Under their reverent observation, night yielded gracefully to day, darkness to light, serenity to splendor.

"It's breathtaking," Holly said.

"People have been watching the sun come up from this platform for over a century," Tim said. "They used to have a bugler who went through the halls waking the guests, and everyone would come running out wrapped in blankets provided by the proprietor."

"Why did they stop?"

Laughter rumbled through his chest. "I guess today's tourists don't appreciate the dawn as much as people did a hundred years ago."

"Fools don't know what they're missing," Holly said.

He chuckled again. "You wouldn't have said that a few minutes ago."

"Morning people!" Holly grumbled.

For several minutes, they stood without moving or speaking, absorbing the beauty and miracle of nature.

"Are you glad you came?" Tim asked.

She turned and slipped her arms around his neck. "Do you have to ask?"

A smile softened his mouth. "Not when I look into your eyes."

He dipped his head to kiss her sweetly, then drew back to look into her eyes again. "When I think how close I came to driving away from your apartment that day without talking to you, it makes my blood run cold."

"I saw you at the door and hid until you walked away. I didn't want to face you."

"But I saw you through the palm fronds, wearing your swimsuit. Your legs—"

Holly grinned. "And I thought you were there because of my eyes."

She nestled her cheek against his chest and sighed thoughtfully as she pondered the way split-second decisions and serendipitous encounters could influence whole lives.

If she'd waited seconds longer to walk back, if he hadn't looked through the palm fronds, if she hadn't accepted his invitation to accompany him to Europe...

So many crossroads. So many places they might have missed each other along the long path that had led them to this rooftop in Austria. So many times either of them could have made rational decisions instead of emotional ones. If she had not trusted Tim's instincts about the fact that he was not married, she might never have fallen in love with him. If he had not trusted his own instincts about the relationship they could have, he might never have asked her to go with him to Europe.

"Come with me, Holly."

A whirlwind trip to Europe had made so little sense. She had been at a disadvantage loving him, yet not knowing whether Tim Sotherland was the man she'd fallen in love with or just a man who laid legitimate claim to the body borrowed by Craig Ford.

"Come with me, Holly."

Had he fully understood what he'd been asking of her? She'd put her job on hold and turned her life upside down with no justification other than the hope that the people they both were inside could find each other again.

"*Come with me, Holly.*"

She so easily could have said no. She had been on the brink of refusing. Then she'd looked into his eyes and recognized the man she saw there, and she'd said yes— yes to Europe, and yes to hope.

What a winding path they'd taken to reach this mountaintop! It seemed like centuries since she'd sat across from him in the café and heard his story of living in a limbo of amnesia, years since she'd stood in his hospital room and realized that he did not recognize her.

Just weeks ago, they'd boarded the plane together as amiable traveling companions, like tourists thrown together on a package tour, excited and curious and a bit apprehensive, awed by the strangeness of the situation in which they'd found themselves. She'd catnapped on the long flight and awakened with her head on his chest, his arm cradling her and his eyes on her face. They'd exchanged self-conscious smiles and stepped back into their roles of intimate strangers.

They'd been painfully courteous to each other in London as they visited Big Ben and Westminster Abbey. Tim had been solicitously attentive in the Tower of London, walking behind her while their shoulders brushed walls that had been touched by monarchs, cupping her elbow at times, prepared to brace her if she stumbled on the ancient stone steps. Afterward, they'd traded cameras and photographed each other on the spot where royal heads had been severed by an executioner's ax.

Like soldiers on a grueling campaign, they'd become allies as they marched through museum after museum, complaining to each other of sore feet and information overload. That evening, at the quaint bed and breakfast they'd chosen over a sleek hotel, they'd been more like old friends as they sat on opposite rims of the huge tub in the community bathroom soaking their feet in hot water and talking about everything and nothing.

The next day, Tim had insisted they go to Madame Tussaud's Wax Museum for a more whimsical perspective on the past and not-so-past. The timbre of their friendship had changed while they stood in front of a macabre exhibit featuring a notorious serial killer. Tim had poked her in the ribs then laughed aloud when she squealed in surprise. At that moment, they'd both known that they had crossed the line between the comfortable familiarity of old friends and the sensual awareness of potential lovers.

Throughout the rest of England, she had shared her passion for books as they toured the homes of great writers, and he'd shared his passion for architecture as they'd explored cathedrals, country churches, castles and town halls.

In Paris, Tim had investigated every arch and ornament of Sacred Heart, Notre Dame and the Arch of Triumph, and she had bought an oil painting from a street artist in Painters' Square. Tim had helped her dicker the price down, using the French he'd learned in college in order to impress a student teaching assistant in the French department.

They'd kissed for the first time atop the Eiffel Tower after watching the sun set, much as they now stood on an Austrian rooftop watching the same sun come up. Holly had felt as though she'd been waiting for that kiss her whole life, just as she now felt she'd waited for this mountainside. Later, they'd taken a moonlight cruise on the Seine, and Tim had whispered French endearments in her ear as the boat slid past couples locked in torrid embraces in the shadows along the bank.

They'd become lovers again that night. Oh how glorious it had been to touch him again! To be touched by him in intimate places. His body was the same one she'd loved and his instincts were the same as always as he made love to her. He had discovered, she had remembered. Together, they had shared the magic.

They'd experienced Germany with the perspective of lovers, finding romance in the quaint ruins of picturesque castles, mountainside vineyards and the legend of the Lorelei Rocks as an excursion boat carried them down the Rhine. They saw Gutenberg's printing press and visited the cathedral at Worms and bought cologne in Cologne. In Rothenburg, they'd driven through an ancient arch where coaches had passed centuries before, and together they'd cringed at the displays of thumbscrews and iron maidens in the Medieval Torture Museum.

Tim had waltzed her through Mad King Ludwig's Hall of Mirrors and whispered naughty suggestions in her ear in Ludwig's grotto. She had bought a cuckoo clock and a wood carving of a mountain climber. Tim had bought several beer steins with pewter caps, and an Alpine mountain climber's hat.

After a thorough inspection of the Oberammergau Cathedral, they'd headed south to Austria, to the historic buildings of Salzburg, to Mozart's home, to the quaint village of Mittenwald, famous for its violins. Then, following narrow winding roads on hillsides so steep they marveled that the dairy cows could keep their footing in the pastures, they'd reached this centuries-old *gasthaus* outside of Bergenz.

They'd shared a lifetime of memories in a matter of weeks.

"Holly."

His voice drew her from deep reflection. His tone was serious. Holly held her breath. Whatever he was going to say was momentous, and she didn't want to miss a syllable.

"If I could hold you like this forever, I would. You'd never be any farther way from me than you are right now."

Holly released the breath she'd been holding and pressed her forehead against his sternum. "I'm not going anywhere."

"Someday, we have to go back to the real world," he said soberly.

"Not today," she said. "Not tomorrow. Not even next week." Down the road, Italy awaited their awe and exploration. The canals of Venice. The Leaning Tower of Pisa. The parks and art of Florence. The ruins, the fountains and cathedrals of Rome. Hand in hand, they would stand in the Sistine Chapel and absorb the splendor of Michelangelo's genius.

"Marry me," he said.

Speechless, Holly tilted her head back so she could see his face.

"The way I feel about you is not going to change, no matter where we go," he said. "I couldn't stop loving you if I tried." He grinned. "Not even a conk on the head could make me forget that I'm not whole without you. I want you with me, here—" He took his arm from around her to place a fist over his heart. "Forever, Holly. Or at least for the rest of our lives."

A moment passed in absolute silence. And absolute perfection. Holly wondered if there would ever be another moment when she felt joy as pure as the joy filling her, spilling over, bathing her like the morning sunlight.

"Holly Bennett, will you marry me?"

She tilted her face up toward his and smiled. "You would ask me when I'm wearing house slippers and a chenille robe!"

"And sexy hair," he said, mussing it playfully, then combing his fingers into the tangled curls to caress her scalp. He kissed her, and the kiss absorbed the perfection of the moment and added to it. It held all the words they didn't need to say and all the feelings they had only to look at each other or touch each other to express.

"Don't I get an answer?"

"Yes."

"Yes, you'll marry me, or yes, I'll get an answer?"

"Yes, I'll marry you," she said.

"I love you, you know."

"Yes," she said, smiling. "I know."

All she had to do was look into his eyes, and she knew it with all her heart.

BRIDE'S BAY RESORT

UNLOCK THE DOOR TO GREAT ROMANCE AT BRIDE'S BAY RESORT

Join Harlequin's new across-the-lines series, set in an exclusive hotel on an island off the coast of South Carolina.

Seven of your favorite authors will bring you exciting stories about fascinating heroes and heroines discovering love at Bride's Bay Resort.

Look for these fabulous stories coming to a store near you beginning in January 1996.

Harlequin American Romance #613 in January
Matchmaking Baby by Cathy Gillen Thacker

Harlequin Presents #1794 in February
Indiscretions by Robyn Donald

Harlequin Intrigue #362 in March
Love and Lies by Dawn Stewardson

Harlequin Romance #3404 in April
Make Believe Engagement by Day Leclaire

Harlequin Temptation #588 in May
Stranger in the Night by Roseanne Williams

Harlequin Superromance #695 in June
Married to a Stranger by Connie Bennett

Harlequin Historicals #324 in July
Dulcie's Gift by Ruth Langan

Visit Bride's Bay Resort each month wherever Harlequin books are sold.

HARLEQUIN ®

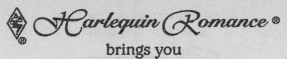

brings you

How the West Was Wooed!

Harlequin Romance would like to welcome you
Back to the Ranch again in 1996 with our new
miniseries, Hitched! We've rounded up twelve of our
most popular authors, and the result is a whole year
of romance, Western-style. Every month we'll be
bringing you a spirited, independent woman whose
heart is about to be lassoed by a rugged, handsome,
one-hundred-percent cowboy!

Watch for books branded Hitched! in the coming
months. We'll be featuring all your favorite
writers including, Patricia Knoll, Ruth Jean Dale,
Rebecca Winters and Patricia Wilson, to mention
a few!

Women throughout time have
lost their hearts to:

Starting in January 1996, Harlequin Temptation
will introduce you to five irresistible, sexy rogues.
Rogues who have carved out their place in history,
but whose true destinies lie in the arms of
contemporary women.

#569 *The Cowboy*, Kristine Rolofson
(January 1996)

#577 *The Pirate*, Kate Hoffmann
(March 1996)

#585 *The Outlaw*, JoAnn Ross
(May 1996)

#593 *The Knight*, Sandy Steen
(July 1996)

#601 *The Highwayman*, Madeline Harper
(September 1996)

Dangerous to love, impossible to resist!

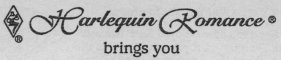

Harlequin Romance ®

brings you

Some men are worth waiting for!

Beginning in January, Harlequin Romance will be
bringing you some of the world's most eligible men.
They're handsome, they're charming, but, best of all,
they're single! Twelve lucky women are about to
discover that finding Mr. Right is not a problem—it's
holding on to him!

In the coming months, watch for our Holding Out for
a Hero flash on books by some of your favorite
authors, including LEIGH MICHAELS, JEANNE ALLAN,
BETTY NEELS, LUCY GORDON and REBECCA WINTERS!

Don't miss out on the fantasy!

We hope you have enjoyed *Secret Fantasies* from Temptation. If you missed any of the books they may be ordered below.

#522	**MEMORY LAPSE**	$3.25 U.S.	☐
	Kathleen O'Brien	$3.75 CAN.	☐
#526	**OBSESSION**	$3.25 U.S.	☐
	Debra Carroll	$3.75 CAN.	☐
#530	**NIGHT GAMES**	$3.25 U.S.	☐
	Janice Kaiser	$3.75 CAN.	☐
#538	**THE MAN FROM SHADOW VALLEY**	$3.25 U.S.	☐
	Regan Forest	$3.75 CAN.	☐
#542	**NIGHTWING**	$3.25 U.S.	☐
	Lynn Michaels	$3.75 CAN.	☐
#546	**NEVER LOVE A COWBOY**	$3.25 U.S.	☐
	Kate Hoffmann	$3.75 CAN.	☐
#550	**NAUGHTY BY NIGHT**	$3.25 U.S.	☐
	Tiffany White	$3.75 CAN.	☐
#554	**STRANGER IN MY ARMS**	$3.25 U.S.	☐
	Madeline Harper	$3.75 CAN.	☐
#558	**KISS OF THE BEAST**	$3.25 U.S.	☐
	Mallory Rush	$3.75 CAN.	☐
#562	**PRIVATE PASSIONS**	$3.25 U.S.	☐
	JoAnn Ross	$3.75 CAN.	☐
#566	**LOOK INTO MY EYES**	$3.25 U.S.	☐
	Glenda Sanders	$3.75 CAN.	☐

(limited quantites available on certain titles)

TOTAL AMOUNT	$
POSTAGE & HANDLING	$
($1.00 for one book, 50¢ for each additional)	
APPLICABLE TAXES*	$ _____
TOTAL PAYABLE	$ _____

(check or money order—please do not send cash)

To order, complete this form and send it, along with a check or money order for the total above, payable to Harlequin Books, to: **In the U.S.:** 3010 Walden Avenue, P.O. Box 9047, Buffalo, NY 14269-9047; **In Canada:** P.O. Box 613, Fort Erie, Ontario, L2A 5X3.

Name: _____

Address: _____ City: _____

State/Prov.: _____ Zip/Postal Code: _____

*New York residents remit applicable sales taxes.
Canadian residents remit applicable GST and provincial taxes.   SFEND

INTRODUCING...

A collection of award-winning books by award-winning authors! From Harlequin and Silhouette.

Falling Angel
by Anne Stuart

WINNER OF THE RITA AWARD
FOR BEST ROMANCE!

Falling Angel by Anne Stuart is a RITA Award winner, voted Best Romance. A truly wonderful story, *Falling Angel* will transport you into a world of hidden identities, second chances and the magic of falling in love.

"Ms. Stuart's talent shines like the brightest of stars, making it very obvious that her ultimate destiny is to be the next romance author at the top of the best-seller charts."
—*Affaire de Coeur*

A heartwarming story for the holidays. You won't want to miss award-winning *Falling Angel,* available this January wherever Harlequin and Silhouette books are sold.

In January, unleash the power
and magic of dreams with

Follow the intriguing lives of:

Kezawin and James—must they deny their love for
fear of an ancient Lakota curse?

Kinnahauk and Bridget—destined to discover a
passion far greater than they'd ever dreamed.

Two complete novels by your favorite authors now
available in one outstanding collection.

MEDICINE WOMAN by Kathleen Eagle
WHITE WITCH by Bronwyn Williams

Their dreams gave them strength.
Their love gave them passion.

Available wherever Harlequin and Silhouette books are sold.